SHORT STORIES

BY

INDIE AUTHORS

VOLUME 4

Short Stories by Indie Authors Volume 4

Cover Design by Pixel Studio

Limited Edition First Print 2021

ISBN: 978-1-7375239-2-5
Published by DEAR Indie Inc.
an organization designed to encourage reading for all ages.
DEARIndie.org

Enter our Annual
Short Story Contest
Entries Accepted
March 1st to July 31st
each year.

Go to

and select Short Story
Contest to enter

The Clock Tower

Mark Piggott

Findley stared at her pocket watch, the moonlight reflecting off the glass. The glow from the dial enabled her to read the time even in the dead of night—four minutes to midnight. Findley worried about the timing as she counted the seconds in her head. *The conjunction lasts one hour. This is my only chance.* Everything had to be done with precision and speed if she was going to reach her objective.

Findley looked at the picture under the lid, a portrait of her with her father, both Foxhares, smartly dressed in pinstripes and ruffles. Their rabbit-like ears and fluffy fox tails stood out in this simple photo. *Sorry, Dad, but this is the only way!*

She stared at the picture of her father and sighed. Her heart fluttered as her mind flooded with fond memories. He taught Findley everything she knew about machinery as a horologist, especially the intricate gears and springs inside a clock. He hoped she would follow in his profession, but Findley used it for other purposes besides repairing timepieces.

Findley was a thief and a good one at that, especially when picking locks or bypassing security systems. She learned her trade on the streets of Alfar City while running with the gangs operating out of the slums hidden in the dark corners of this theocratic militant state. She made exquisite machines for each job, sometimes selling her tools of the trade to the highest bidder for a cut of the take. Findley was considered one of the best in the business for someone barely in her twenties.

Tonight, though, it was different. This evening, under the moonlit sky, Findley watched and waited for her chance . . . an opportunity at redemption and the ultimate prize. She closed the watch, tucked it away, and studied the objective from her rooftop perch. It stood over 500 meters tall, with an imposing steel and stone structure. The lofty parapets, disfigured gargoyles, pointed arches, and flying buttresses offset the gothic tower by the giant clock face on the north facade.

It was called the Clock Tower, but this spire was more than a mere timepiece. The throne of the monarchy, the treasure vault, and the central prison were all under one roof inside this massive structure. When someone said they were going to the clock tower, you never knew whether the outcome would be good or bad.

The tower cast a massive shadow over the heart of Alfar City, like the hand of a sundial, telling time by sunlight and moonlight. With three moons throwing light over the world, they never knew what true darkness was, but Findley knew that would change tonight. Alfar City would be engulfed in the blackest night, a void of eternal darkness.

As the daughter of a horologist, Findley understood the relationship between time, the moons' phases, and the stars' alignment. Many clocks and timepieces often displayed both time and astrological movements, making celestial mapping an essential tool of the trade. She knew all about the coming convergence—when the largest moon, Ymir, would eclipse the two smaller moons, Baldur and Freyr. It would only last an hour—but that was all the time Findley needed.

She pulled the hood of her cloak over her ears, drawing it around her face. Findley stayed in the shadows, avoiding the gaze of the tower guards—Owlbears. These demihumans were often used as soldiers and security due to their ferocity, guile, and tenacity. They had excellent noses for detecting intruders but terrible eyesight in low light. Findley hoped to take advantage of that when she began her assault on the clock tower.

She looked up in the sky and watched as the conjunction began its dance amongst the stars. The moons inched closer with every passing minute as a giant shadow fell across the city, and then it happened. The convergence engulfed Alfar City in absolute darkness. Findley heard the screams and cries of the people below as panic set in. Lights went on in every building, but the illumination only brightened the ground-level cityscape. The clock tower remained dark as the light below could not reach the massive structure.

Findley stepped to the roof's edge and pulled her goggles over her eyes. She adjusted the optics, slowly tuning the lenses until her eyesight adjusted to the total darkness covering the tower. A soft green light glowed from the lenses and illuminated her surroundings. The handmade night-vision goggles worked perfectly.

She stepped up on the ledge, carefully keeping a sure footing on the stone outcropping. She examined the clock tower closely until she found her target—a balcony protruding from the structure nearly halfway up the spire. It belonged to Marquis du Crémant, the king's advisor. In a situation like the convergence, his duty was to be with the king. That meant his office should be empty, allowing Findley to sneak into the tower. The hard part was getting up there.

Without hesitation, Findley fell forward, plummeting toward the ground. She dropped like a rock, trying to pick up speed while counting the seconds as the ground inched closer and closer. With seconds to spare, Findley pulled a ripcord from under her cloak. Gears clicked and turned as springs forcibly ejected a pair of wings from within her backpack. The bat-like wings of aurilite tubing and woven fabric caught the air. Findley swerved upwards, gliding right along the side of the clock tower.

She had practiced this maneuver for weeks in the canyons north of Alfar City, searching for months until she had found a place resembling the height and spacing between the tower and the surrounding buildings. Her research and relentless practice were about to pay off.

Except, Findley realized she might not reach her destination. The air currents generated by her fall pushed her higher and higher up the side of the clock tower, but as she closed in on the marquis's balcony, she began to slow down. *It must be the difference in the air currents between here and the canyon!*

Deep down, her heart began to race, but Findley knew better than to panic. Fear wasn't a beneficial asset for a thief, so she made a quick decision. She released the rip-cord, causing the wings to retract back into the backpack. *I can do this!* She repeated the mantra in her head. *The talons should work!*

Her momentum kept her going toward the tower wall, and right before she hit, Findley reached out for the wall. She opened her hand and flexed her wrist, activating a mechanism within her gloves. Sharp claws of dimonium steel popped open and extended more than two inches from her fingertips. She used the last of her flying momentum to lunge at the tower, latching onto it with all her strength.

Findley gripped the stone wall, desperately trying to get her footing, but the smooth stone made that nearly impossible. Realizing it was necessary to deploy her second countermeasure, she clicked her heels together. A three-inch dimonium blade popped out from the tip of her boots. She kicked as hard as she could, burying the edge into the stone.

That was close! Too close for comfort! She breathlessly exhaled as beads of sweat trickled down her face.

Findley stopped for a minute to get her bearings, exhilarated and terrified, as she glimpsed at the sheer drop beneath her. She took a couple of deep breaths and then slowly began her climb, ensuring her grip and footing were secure with each move up the wall. She had less than fifty feet to reach the balcony, but it seemed like a mile to her.

Time was limited. Findley hurried along her ascent as best as she could. When she reached the balcony, she could hear voices coming from inside the marquis's office. She dug her nails into the edge of the balcony and pulled herself up to peer over the edge. The light inside the office shone brightly through two large glass and metal doors, nearly blinding Findley in her night-vision gear. She closed her eyes, gripping the ledge with one hand and raising her goggles with the other. Once adjusted, she glanced over again until the doors swung open.

A tall, lanky Vorrat stepped out, quickly pulling a silk robe tight over a ruffled shirt. Findley recognized his large nose and floppy ears, his stringy hair pulled back into a ponytail, and the sickly-sweet scent of perfume that filled the air. Vorrats were well known for their cunning and intellect, something Marquis du Crémant excelled in. He rushed to the balcony, staring into the darkness above him before looking across Alfar City. His sensitive ears could pick up the sounds of terror from every corner, which deeply concerned him.

"Marquis!" an Owlbear guard shouted as he followed behind the marquis. The musketlance clanged off the floor as he charged through the door with each step. Nearly seven feet tall, a mass of fur and feathers under plate armor, the Owlbear towered over the Vorrat. "Marquis du Crémant, Her Majesty, Queen Lilibeth, wants to see you immediately! The disappearance of the moons vexes her!"

"It's called an eclipse, you idiot!" he corrected the guard as he stared up into the night sky. "The three moons are aligned in a perfect convergence that blocks all light in the evening sky. It's incredible. They only happen once in a lifetime. Why didn't my scientific advisors inform me of the possibility?"

"Will it end, or are we cursed in this darkness forever?"

"Fear not, my muscle-bound cretin, it will soon pass," Marquis said, glancing over the balcony to the ground below. "Are there any security breaches to the tower that I should know about?"

"No, my lord, but people are beginning to storm the main gate as we speak, clamoring for answers. I've doubled the security forces there."

"Good. For now, let's go reassure our hysterical queen that this will soon be over," the marquis growled before storming off the balcony. The guard started to follow but stopped for a moment, sniffing deep as a scent caught his attention. He returned to the balcony, snorting loudly as he tried to locate the strange smell.

Findley worried it might have caught her scent. She took

every precaution to ensure she left no lingering odor on her person, including washing herself and her clothes with vinegar. It should have done the trick, but Owlbears had such sensitive nostrils that one never knew. Findley lowered herself back down from the balcony, moving under the lip of the edge.

The Owlbear gripped onto the balcony rail, peering over the side, snorting loudly as it tried to find that elusive scent.

"What are you waiting for, you imbecile? An invitation?" Marquis du Crémant shouted from inside his room, startling the guard back to his senses. He huffed before rushing back to follow the marquis.

Findley waited a moment, listening closely until she heard the door close behind them. Cautiously, she pulled herself onto the balcony, laying low as she crawled across the floor on her belly. She peered through the glass doors, checking if the room was empty. With her talons retracted, Findley quickly and quietly got to her feet and tiptoed across the room. Breathlessly, she watched for any movement in the light shining from under the door.

Findley pulled out her pocket watch to check her timing. *Five minutes behind schedule*, she mused silently before moving on. *The convergence will only last for another forty minutes. I must get into the clockwork before it ends.*

She tucked her watch away and scanned the room. There were paintings and busts of Marquis du Crémant scattered about the room. This man's over-inflated ego made Findley dislike him even more. As she continued her search, Findley spotted what she was looking for—a ventilation grating positioned directly above the marquis's desk.

The marquis's room was in the top section of the clock tower. The central ventilation shaft, circulating fresh air inside the building, was above her and went all the way to the clockwork. It was a shortcut, a dangerous one, but the fastest way up there.

Findley climbed on the desk and reached into her tool belt. After carefully removing the grate with a screwdriver, she gazed up into the ventilation shaft. Her hair tussled about from the intense downdraft. The cold air sent a shiver down her spine. Findley decided to put the grate into a desk drawer, wondering if they would think to look for it there or even notice it was missing.

After extending her talons again, Findley jumped into the shaft, digging into the metal as she pulled herself inside. She crawled through the shaft, quite a snug fit, but Findley squeezed through until she reached the main shaft. It was a fifty-foot square vertical shaft that rose hundreds of feet to the top of the tower. The problem was what lay between.

Massive horizontal fans kept the shaft in a constant downdraft. Fresh air was pulled from the top of the tower and circulated throughout the building below. Those fans were the only thing that stood between Findley and the clockwork at the top.

The force of the air blowing through the shaft was fierce. Findley fought against the swirling winds, struggling to stay on her feet until she reached the wall. Slowly, she crouched down and went into her backpack, pulling out a small robotic flying fish.

"Okay, Skipper, time to go to work!"

The mechanism resembled a simple toy with articulated wings of copper wire and a flexible polymer. With the touch of a button, a mass of gears and springs came to life as it fluttered like a hummingbird's wings. She let it go, and the mechanical fish flew toward the first fan. It circled the shaft, slowly rising through the air like a tiny robotic fish swimming against the current. Once there, electrical sparks shot out from its mouth and into the engine. The fan sputtered and slowed as the power surge traveled up the shaft along the conduits, suddenly causing all to stop spinning.

Expending all its energy, the little fish dropped from the air. Findley leaped to her feet to catch her valuable tool. "Good boy, Skipper!" She patted it on its head before tucking it back in her backpack. Now came the hard part of getting up the shaft as quickly as possible. With the fans shorted out, she should be able to get up to the clockwork. Findley had invented just the tool to help her reach her goal—a pneumatic harpoon gun.

She unholstered her ascension gun from her hip. It contained a compressed air canister with a hooked piton in the chamber connected to a coil of dimonium steel line. She opened the valve to prime the weapon before carefully aiming at the fan housing above. Findley knew she could climb the walls using her talons, but that would take too much time. Traversing the air shaft this way was much easier and more fun.

She fired the piton, launching it into the fan as the line spun out from the housing. Once the piton locked in, Findley flipped a second switch, and the coil retracted, pulling her up through the air until she reached the first fan. She climbed to the next level before unhooking the piton and repeating the process. Findley came to the third fan, with only two sections remaining, when she heard a familiar sound—the fan motors started to re-engage.

What? They're rebooting the system! This should have been a low priority, unless . . . Findley cursed under her breath when she realized her mistake. She didn't anticipate them restarting the fans in the ventilation shaft so soon. The fear stoked by the convergence might have panicked the royal family, so their comfort would be prioritized.

Findley had to act fast; once the fans reached full power, the force of the downdraft could push her back down the shaft or into the other blades. She aimed past the next fan toward the last one at the top of the air shaft. It took nearly the entire length of the dimonium line, but the piton finally locked into place.

She flipped the switch and started her ascent. Findley gritted her teeth tighter with each passing moment. *Hurry, hurry!* Her mind raced through the myriad of calculations to calm her nerves and, in part, pray for a miracle. Unfortunately, her prayer wasn't answered. The fan kicked in and spun about, flinging the helpless thief around the shaft. Findley locked the spindle so she wouldn't get pulled into the blades, but it only worsened things. As the motor picked up speed, it flung her mercilessly around as her grip began to weaken on the handle of her ascension gun.

Findley only had a slight chance to survive. She spied a small side shaft leading off the main about thirty feet down. She had no idea where it led, only that she had no choice.

Timing it just right, Findley used the momentum of her spin to swing into the smaller ventilation shaft. As she slid in, she snapped the line and freed the piton, her speed banging her around the tiny vent. Without warning, the shaft curved, and she crashed through a grate, falling into another room.

Findley landed hard, her head bouncing against the floor. She was momentarily disoriented, her eyes needing to adjust to the new surroundings. When everything focused, she noticed the room was pink and pastel-colored. Ruffles, overstuffed pillows, and various stuffed animals and dolls were scattered about the rather messy room.

It was then Findley noticed a pair of eyes staring down at her. They belonged to a young female Liger, one of the noblest breeds of demi-humans, with a flowing mane of multi-colored striped hair of white, orange, and black, sharp ears, and a wispy tail. Surrounding all that strength and nobility was even more pink ruffles in a frock underneath a tiny crown of gold and jewels.

Findley recognized her immediately—Princess Treena Meghaan Sharona Regalia, the one and only heir to the crown of Alfar City. The ten-year-old was the people's darling, quite popular among all the nobles in the royal family.

"Hello!" said the little princess, staring at Findley with big green eyes. "Are you alright? You took a nasty fall from the ceiling."

Findley slowly rolled over and pushed herself to a sitting position, but even that was difficult. Her head was still dizzy from the impact. She didn't know what to say or how to act in front of Her Royal Highness. She feared the little princess might alert the guards, but for some reason, Findley sensed more concern than fear from the little girl.

"Here, drink some dramberry juice. It'll make you feel better," Treena said, rushing over to her table to get a glass for Findley. "They always bring me some at bedtime, but you can have it. I can always ask for more."

The little princess handed her the glass of juice. Findley took it gingerly, unsure of the situation or how to act around the little princess. "Thank you, Your Highness," Findley replied before taking a sip. The sweet nectar did the trick, as the sugar rush alleviated the throbbing pain in her head.

"What's your name?"

Findley paused before responding, wondering if she should tell the princess her real name. She was a real charmer, and it was against her better judgment to tell her the truth. As a thief, anonymity is your best friend. It was a strange feeling, but deep down, her instincts told Findley that she could trust the little girl. Something in her eyes—an innocence with a glint of mild apprehension—stirred her troubled heart. Somehow, Findley knew she could put her faith in the little princess.

"Findley," she uttered. "Findley Doyle."

"It's very nice to meet you, Findley," Treena said with a curtsey. "I guess you know who I am, don't you?"

"Of course, Your Highness. It's an honor to meet you."

"I don't get many visitors, just servants, tutors, and nannies. I usually don't receive guests falling through the ventilation system either," Treena added. "Is there something you need to tell me, or should I just call for the guards?"

Findley realized this little princess was far more intelligent than she appeared. "To be honest, Princess Treena, I'm here to find something my father left behind in the clockwork."

"Your father?" Treena asked. "What do you mean?"

Findley spun her story to the little princess. Her father, Obadiah Doyle, was one of the clockmakers assigned to construct the clockwork within the tower. He worked diligently on fine-tuning the gears, springs, and timing mechanisms to ensure the clock worked to perfection. During his work, while installing one of the jeweled movements of the clock, his watchchain broke, and he lost his pocket watch within the clock mechanism. Obadiah could not recover it, and when he asked to look for it, his petition was denied by Marquis du Crémant. It seemed the marquis didn't want to waste time looking for a sentimental timepiece and refused. Plus, he was always a distrusting soul, especially of commoners trying to get into the clock tower. Her father had repeatedly requested to go into the clock but was always denied. When his health started failing, Findley made the requests on his behalf, but she was also rejected.

"That's why I decided to break into the tower tonight," Findley concluded, handing the empty juice glass back to the princess. "I knew the convergence would be my last chance to get his watch back for him."

"Well, if you don't mind me asking, it's a simple pocket watch. Why is it so important for you to risk your life for a trinket like that?" Treena inquired as she set the glass down. Findley sighed, realizing the truth behind her question and understanding why something like a pocket watch would seem so insignificant to a member of royalty.

"It was the last thing my mother gave my father before she died." Findley clenched her fists tightly to control her temper. "It's all he has left of her. Ever since he lost it, he's been sick and dying. I think he's dying of a broken heart."

Her answer caught Princess Treena by surprise. Findley watched as the little princess touched the bracelet on her wrist, probably a gift from her mother. Findley knew she understood the relationship between a parent and their child.

"I know I have no right to ask this of you, but I am begging you, Your Highness," Findley began, bowing her head reverently to the little princess. "I'm not here to steal anything of wealth or value to the kingdom. All I want is to get my father's watch back. Please, let me continue my mission before the convergence ends."

Treena thought for a minute and then smiled and chuckled. "It sounds like a great adventure! Let's go!" The little princess jumped to her feet and started walking over to her wardrobe. Her sudden pronouncement caught Findley off guard.

"Go where?" she sputtered.

"To the clockwork, of course." Treena twisted a handle on her wardrobe, causing the massive piece of furniture to slide open and reveal a secret passage. "It's my favorite place to view the city from."

Findley was shocked to see a secret passage, something her research never uncovered. "What is this, Your Highness?"

"The servants use these stairs to move up and down the tower," Treena explained. "I use it to sneak up to the clockwork from time to time. It's great fun!"

"Your Highness!" Findley exclaimed, grabbing the little princess by the shoulder. "I can't ask you to help me in my endeavors. I don't want to get you in trouble."

Treena smiled slightly and replied, "But I like trouble; it's more fun that way! Besides, I want to help set things right. By helping you, I am helping your father get better."

Findley was touched by the kind sincerity of the little princess as a tear welled up in her eye. "Thank you, Your Highness. This means a lot to me."

"Please stop being so formal, Findley." The little princess clasped her hands around Findley's. "You can call me Treena." Her brilliant smile and bright eyes were intoxicating. Findley knew this princess had a great future ahead of her.

The two ran up the stairs, rushing past each step until they reached the top. Treena pushed open another secret door, and they stepped out into the clockwork. The sound was deafening inside the massive clock, from the constant ratcheting of the gears to the pendulum's sway to a melodic beat. It was grace and precision in action, leaving Findley in awe.

Treena looked outside through one of the glass shutters and then tugged on Findley's cloak to get her attention. The stars were the only thing they could see shining through the darkness. The city was still engulfed in the convergence. "It's still dark outside. How much longer is this going to last?" she asked.

Findley pulled out her pocket watch and calculated the minutes. "Less than twelve minutes left," she replied. "I've got to hurry."

"Where was your father working when he lost his watch?"

"In the back of the clock, near the jeweled movement," Findley pointed, rushing around the back of the clockwork.

"What's a jeweled movement?" Princess Treena asked, rushing to follow her.

"Clockmakers sometimes use precious stones in place of metal parts to reduce the wear and tear caused by friction," Findley explained, pointing up to the main bearing. It was a spindle of selenium ruby, the toughest and most precious gemstone known in the land. Jewelers and horologists prized the selenium ruby for its beauty, luster, and durability. "A jeweled spindle like that will last years longer than a simple metal one."

Treena looked at the mechanics in awe. She hung on Findley's every word of the clock's inner workings. "So, where's your father's watch?"

"It should be sitting on one of the horizontal gears near the escape wheel," Findley explained, taking off her backpack and setting it down.

"Well, how do you get up there? It must be a hundred feet up?"

Ignoring the little princess's question, Findley pulled out a couple of mechanical fish. Princess Treena looked at the robotic fish with curiosity.

"What are those?"

"This is Gilligan and the Professor." Findley held out the two devices in her hands. "They're my heavy lifters."

"What are they going to lift?" Treena asked.

"Me!" Findley said as she flipped the switches, activating the fluttering wings of the flying fish. The two of them hovered close to the ground. Findley stepped on top of each one, carefully getting her balance. She gripped a handheld controller, flipped a couple of switches, and then used her thumb to control the joystick. Slowly, Findley began to rise in the air, up toward the escape wheel and the associated gears.

Findley could see the little princess's eyes light up as she floated into the air. She carefully manipulated the toggles and switches to position herself between and near the gears. Raising herself a little higher, she looked around each gear to find what she was looking for. She watched as the jeweled spindle precisely measured each tick on the clock.

And there was the pocket watch, opened, sitting precariously on the spinning gear. It spun around in a circle like a ballerina on tiptoes. Findley watched her mother's picture under the watch lid dance as it turned on the gear. To the young Foxhare, it was like looking in a mirror. She saw her own eyes staring back at her.

Findley reached over and picked up the watch. Her heart skipped a beat as she showed it to Princess Treena, waving it proudly. The little princess applauded, jumping up and down, happy that Findley retrieved her family heirloom with relative ease.

Suddenly, the two were startled by the sounds of footsteps rushing into the clockwork. Treena ran around to see what was going on, leaving Findley on her own as she started her descent to the floor.

Findley kept an eye on Treena as the little princess moved cautiously across the floor. Princess Treena told Findley about all the ways in and out of the clock tower. The Owlbears patrolled on a strict schedule, and this sudden appearance wasn't planned.

Her heart skipped a beat when she suddenly realized why. Findley spied Marquis du Crémant stepping out onto the floor with several Owlbears. The princess stopped in her tracks and headed back toward Findley just as she landed. She quickly packed her robotic fish into her backpack as Treena turned the corner.

"Findley! Marquis du Crémant is here!" she breathlessly warned her. "You've got to leave! Follow me; I know another way out!"

Findley slung her backpack over her shoulders and followed her close behind. Still, they were cut off by two Owlbears, leveling their musketlances, frightening them both. More Owlbears came up from behind, boxing them into a corner. Findley stood in front of the princess, protecting her from the menacing guards.

"Well, now, this is quite surprising," a voice echoed from behind the Owlbears as Marquis du Crémant stepped forward. "I'm impressed you made it to the top of the clock tower. You might have gotten away with it, but your poor filing skills gave you away." He tossed the vent cover at her feet, letting it rattle off the floor. Findley realized her mistake in stuffing it in the marquis's desk instead of reattaching it.

"Now, I'm afraid we'll be making your stay in the tower more permanent a . . ." The marquis stuttered and stumbled with his words when he finally noticed Princess Treena peeking out from behind Findley. "P-P-Princess Treena? Your Highness, what are you doing here? And with this . . . thief?"

Treena cleared her throat and stepped out from behind Findley. The marquis stood defiant, waiting patiently for the little royal to answer him. The Owlbears immediately raised their weapons and dropped to one knee, bowing their heads before Her Royal Highness.

"I came here to help Findley find her father's pocket watch, Marquis du Crémant. She asked for my help, and I gave it to her, something you should have done in the first place!" The little princess stood firm, scolding the marquis for his inaction. Even one of the Owlbears chuckled at this tiny girl admonishing the tower administrator.

"Your Highness, I don't know what this reprobate told you, but it does not excuse her breaking into the tower nor assisting this thief in her criminal activities. Really, what would your parents say?"

Frightened at the thought of having to explain this to her parents, Princess Treena was at a loss for words until she felt a reassuring hand on her shoulder. Findley reached out to comfort her newfound friend.

"It's alright, Your Highness. I told you before; I don't want you to get in trouble," she reassured her. "I have to take responsibility for what I did tonight."

Findley knew Treena didn't want to disappoint her new friend. She went into this knowing that she could get into trouble for helping Findley. The princess was known for having a bit of a rebellious streak, but this was a little bigger than sticking your tongue out at the ambassador from Sephora.

Treena nodded at Findley but looked at the marquis with sheer contempt before she moved even an inch from her side. "I want your word, Marquis du Crémant. Findley will not be charged with anything associated with me. I came here of my own free will."

The Marquis gritted his teeth at this little girl making demands of him, but he had no choice but to acquiesce as long as she wore the crown. "You have my word, Your Highness. I will not charge her with anything to do with your being here."

Treena gave a loud gruff as she raised her nose to the marquis and walked away from Findley, stepping between the Owlbears. Once the princess was safe, Marquis du Crémant turned his attention to Findley.

"Now, then, seize her and lock her up. We'll let His Majesty decide her fate once he finds out she kidnapped Princess Treena."

Treena was taken aback by the marquis's announcement. "But you gave me your word!"

"I said that *I* would not charge her with the crime of kidnapping, Your Highness. I did not say your father could not charge her. Such are the whims of a monarch desperate to protect the future queen of Alfar City. Now, arrest her!"

Just as the Owlbears leveled their musketlances at Findley, the sly Foxhare went into action. She threw down a couple of foxfire grenades, which exploded with a brilliant flash of glittery light and a plume of smoke that filled the air. The fumes from the foxfire scorched the inside of Owlbear's noses, causing them to cough and sneeze violently. She then pulled out a quick-sealing respirator and slapped it over her face, and grabbed two more of her flying fish. Quick as could be, Findley tossed them into the air toward the guards.

"Let's go, Ginger and Mary Ann! Clear a path for me!" she shouted. The robotic fish buzzed toward two Owlbears, their beating wings cutting into their armor and flesh. These mechanical fish buzzed with razor-sharp wings. The Owlbears separated, leaving a clear path for Findley to charge right through them.

"Stop her, you idiots!" the marquis shouted as he continued sneezing and coughing from the foxfire, but it was too late. Findley leaped through one of the clockface shutters, plummeting headfirst toward the ground. Everyone rushed over to the window to see what had happened to her.

The convergence ended as quickly as it began, and the moon's light illuminated Alfar City again, bringing it out of the endless darkness. It was then that they saw her, with wings spread from beneath her backpack, flying across the rooftops toward the city's outskirts, swooping down toward the slums and home.

Findley thought she saw a flash of a smile and a wave from the little princess behind the glass as she flew across the cityscape. That little Liger was a lightning rod, a tempered metal that could take on anything the gods threw at her, including the fury of Marquis du Crémant. She hoped the marquis wouldn't take out his frustrations on Princess Treena, but deep down, she knew Treena would be just fine.

The one thing Findley knew implicitly was time and patience. She knew it would take them years before they discovered the selenium ruby spindle missing from the clock. It would take time for the aurilite spindle she replaced it with to wear down and break, causing the clock to fail. By that time, Findley and her father would be sequestered far away from Alfar City, with new identities and a new life, maybe somewhere by the sea. They'd be able to live easily off the money she'd make fencing the spindle.

She thought about spending some of her earnings on a present for Princess Treena to thank her for the help. She would watch the clock tower and watch for Her Royal Highness to sneak up there once more. When she decided to pay another visit to the clockwork, Findley would send the little princess a flying fish of her own. That would be fun.

"I think I'll call it Minnow!" she pondered as she flew toward her father and home. He would be angry with her for risking her life and breaking into the clock tower, but in the end, he would do like he always did and relent. Besides, seeing his precious watch again would make him smile. Findley lived for that.

The End

Why I Wrote this Story:

My sister, Trina, died in 2021. Her sudden death hit everyone hard, especially her daughter, Meghan. They both loved Disney and the time they spent there together, so I wrote this story and turned them into a princess. That way, mother and daughter will always be together.

LEO

Robert John DeLuca

The little girl clung to her mother's arm as the train bumped along. She hardly glanced at the green fields, villages, and distant hills that flew by. She was sad, very sad. Home was back there. She might never see it again. They had been riding for two days after rushing to the station to join the masses of women and children desperate to escape from their village. Her mother had shaken her awake while it was still dark and told her to get dressed. They must leave. The Russians were coming. She heard booms like thunder that seemed way off until her house and the earth under it shook violently with a tremendous crash and explosion that was much closer.

She heard her daddy say to mommy, "I think it hit a few blocks over. Please hurry.

The next train for Poland leaves in fifteen minutes. I have tickets for you and Nina."

"But Anton, surely you are coming with us? It is much too dangerous to remain here", Sofia pleaded, her eyes glistening in the sparsely lit light of their living room.

"No, darling," he replied. "My place, for now, is here in our village with the men. We need to fight these invaders and defend our homes. We are strong and determined. You'll see. In just a few days, I'll be asking you to return. For now, we must think about Nina above all else. You must take her away from here."

Sofia held her husband's gaze for a moment and then rushed into his arms. He was right, of course. They must get their eight-year-old daughter away before the Russian tanks came rolling into town. She squeezed him as hard as she could and then turned away to see what was keeping their little princess.

Nina stuffed some clothes in her backpack and was sitting on her bed with Leo, her best friend in the world. The black and white beagle mix had his head on her lap, with his floppy ears spread on each leg. She was scratching him as his big dark eyes continently looked up at her. They'd had the stout, short-legged pup for about a year, after the scruffy little creature came bouncing out of the weeds in their backyard. Ignoring her mother's warnings about stray animals, Nina ran over and picked him up. His tail was wagged, and he covered her with kisses. Anton made a half -hearted effort to find the stray's owner with no success. Leo became a family member in short order. Nina did not want to leave her best friend behind.

"Come on, Nina. Daddy is waiting. Say goodbye to Leo, and hurry or we will miss the train."

The little girl hugged the dog. "I'm not going without Leo! Can we take him with us?" On cue, the little dog rolled over and whimpered to have his tummy rubbed. On most occasions, his cuddly charm won the day, but not this time

"No. We can't take him on a crowded train. It is not permitted. We are not sure what lies ahead for us. He'll be fine here with daddy. We should be able to return soon. He'll be okay."

Nina, who was known for her terrible meltdowns, decided that her mother was right. As much as she loved Leo, he would be better off here. She reached down and rubbed his furry tummy and said, "Leo, you be a good boy for daddy. We'll be back soon." With tears streaming down her face and a lump in her throat, she took her mother's hand and walked out of the bedroom. Leo trotted faithfully next to them as far as he could. Nina

could see his little black nose, floppy ears, and sad eyes looking out the window behind the living room curtains as they drove away in daddy's car.

The station was choked with people waiting to board the train to Poland. Stanovia was a country village far from any large city. Most everyone who lived there knew everyone else. Still, those who were leaving were eager to get on the train. There was a lot of pushing and shoving. Tempers were short. Anton parked as close as he could. He picked up Sofia's bag in one hand and his daughter in the other. With his wife just behind him, he worked his way through the crowd. He was a big man and that helped him to reach the steps of the railcar, where a conductor was attempting to keep order and prevent people without tickets from rushing on board.

Anton held up the rail pass. The man nodded and took Nina in his arms and helped her up the steps. He then offered his hand to Sofia, who followed. There was no time for hugs, kisses, or proper goodbyes. Anton did not know if he would ever see them again. He just stood there, numb to what he had just done. He let himself be pushed along by the crowd, incredibly saddened by their leaving. There was the unmistakable successive banging of hitches as the train lurched forward. He looked up as the windows rolled slowly by. He thought he saw Nina's little face pressed against the glass, but he couldn't be sure. The train gathered speed and disappeared into the distance. He had never felt so alone in his life.

The train ride was boring. They were crammed in their seats with nowhere to go. There was always a line at the potty. The train was hot for a while and then it became cold and then hot again. Like any youngster on a trip, at least once an hour Nina asked her

mother, Are we there yet? Sofia took these questions with good humor and was careful to comfort rather than upset her daughter.

Nina thought about Leo and hoped he was okay. Did daddy know how much to feed him, and that he ate twice a day? She hoped daddy wouldn't be too busy to let him out after he ate. She wondered where he would sleep. He always curled up at the foot of her bed. Would he do that if she were not there? Maybe he would go into daddy's room. She loved little Leo, and she knew he loved her as well. She couldn't imagine life without him, but how good are dogs at remembering people?

With her voice cracking, she asked her mommy, "Of course, I miss daddy, but I also love Leo. If we are gone for very long, do you think he will forget me? Will he know me when we go back home?"

Her mother reached over and pulled her close. "Leo will never forget you. He can't wait to see you again. Dogs love their masters forever. He is just as eager to see you as you are to see him."

She felt a little better about things after talking to her mom. She drifted off into such a deep sleep that she did not notice it when the train heaved to a final stop: Poland. They followed the crowd into the station and got in line at an immigration booth. They reached a man in a uniform, who inspected their papers and asked a few questions. He then stamped their papers. Sofia did not know where to go next, other than to get out of the way of the line behind her.

When they got outside, a kindly lady wearing an armband approached them. She pointed to a large tent in the parking lot across the street with a banner that read

"Welcome to Poland." "Walk over to that tent. we have food and drink and people who can help you find a place to stay," she said with a smile.

Sofia thanked her. Sure enough, in the tent there were sandwiches, bags of chips, soft drinks, sweet rolls, and hot coffee. They did not realize how hungry they were and laughed as they agreed this was their best meal ever. Nina broke off a small corner of her sandwich for Leo, as she always did. She fought back tears when she realized he wasn't there. Oh, how she missed her best friend.

A man came around and took their names. Local citizens were accepting refugees into their homes. He asked them to remain nearby and hoped to have a place for them in a few hours. No problem, as there was nowhere else to go.

True to his word, the fellow called their names two hours later. He was standing next to a large lady who wore wire-rimmed glasses, a long straight dress, and thick high laced shoes. She had a stern look on her face. The man introduced them to Pan Kohler, who had an empty loft they might use for a while.

Pan Kohler looked them over with a critical eye. She then demanded, "Just two? No men. No boys. No boyfriends. No pets. No sickness. No COVID. No drinking. No smoking. No drugs. No loud music."

Sofia was overwhelmed, but assured the woman, the two of them complied with her list. The woman actually walked around them twice more.

Finally, she pointed to a battered old Volvo parked down the street. "Okay, come with me."

Under most circumstances, Sofia would have told this officious woman to bug off, but she had no choice but to follow her to her car. It was good that she did. As things turned out, Pan Kohler had a comfortable place that suited Sofia and Nina perfectly. Despite her outward demeanor, she was warm and gracious.

Back home, Leo was not himself. He missed Nina. When she returned home from school, he followed her everywhere. He had a basket full of dog toys. He'd pull one out and drop at her feet and pant anxiously for her to toss it for him to chase. When Leo first came to live with them, her mother agreed he could stay with one hard and fast rule, "No animals on the furniture. No exceptions!" Leo broke that rule in about thirty seconds as he curled up with Nina on the couch as she watched cartoons. Mommy also had a rule about little girls eating everything on their plate at dinner. Leo stationed himself on the floor within the drop zone of Nina's meal, just in case something came his way. The little animal would eat anything except blueberries.

"Okay, boy", Anton said as he returned from the station. "It's just you and me now.

I know you miss them. I do too."

The little dog ran to the front window and looked out to where Anton's truck was parked. Where were Nina and Sofia? He then scrambled around the house and checked every room. Finally, he walked up to Anton, who was sitting in his easy chair, and gave him a quizzical look. Anton shrugged, partly because he did not want to break down. Leo sensed what was up and flopped next to him on the floor. The guys would make it through this. They had to.

The next morning, Anton went into town for a meeting of the civil defense group that hoped to stop the Russian advance, which was fast approaching. The men were armed with hunting rifles and shotguns, which would be no match for the Russian tanks and machine guns. Still, local pride was high. The group would not surrender Stanovia without a fight.

One man stood up and said, "I will never give up. Stanovia is my home. It was my parents' home and their parents before that. I am prepared to fight these invaders to the death!"

A round of "Yes! Yes!" erupted from the men. There was no question they would fight to the last man.

When the cheering stopped, the mayor, an older man, spoke in a level tone. "Men, I admire your spirit and your hearts. I feel the same as you do, but we must be reasonable. We are not a combat ready force. We have no training or equipment. Whether or not we resist, the Russians can flatten our little village in an eye blink. We are so insignificant. I don't think they will waste much time here. I think the best approach is to stand down and let them pass through. If we fight them, we may hold them off for a while, but they will surely overwhelm us. I believe the smart thing to do right now is lie low. They probably won't even notice us."

There was much grumbling among the men, but in the end, they knew what he suggested was best. They disbursed without agreeing to mount an organized resistance. Anton returned home anxious about what the next few days would bring. Leo was always happy to see him and had taken to snoozing next to his bed. Anton discovered more and more he was discussing problems with the little pooch, who was a good listener.

Although cell service was spotty, Anton had talked to his wife and daughter. He was relieved they had made it without incident and found a place to stay. He assured them everything was fine at home, and yes, he and Leo were getting along famously. In fact, the dog followed him whenever he went and was excited to see him when he returned home from work.

Two days later, the hated Russians rolled into town. Their tanks rumbled through the village square and infantry troops followed on the ground. When Anton saw how many there were, he was glad the mayor had spoken. The Russians stopped long enough only to rip down the local flag and raise theirs in the town square.

Anton held his breath as he stood in his doorway, peeking out at the long column of troops and supplies filing past his house. It looked like the mayor had been right. Stanovia might escape the destruction, after all. Just as it looked like the end of the line was near, he saw a tiny blur dart across the front of his house, right into the Russian column. Oh no! Leo, get back here! The obsessed beagle had other plans. He attacked the first foot soldier he came to and grabbed his leg, chewing and howling for all he was worth. The surprised man fell over and Leo bit the man's arm, drawing blood. When several other soldiers came to the rescue, Leo scampered back to his house, where Anton stood in shock.

The damage had been done. As Anton watched horrified, an enormous tank fell out of line. Its turret pivoted and its cannon cranked down level with his house. Before Anton could react, his house exploded in a tremendous boom, burst of fire, and debris. The Russians would not tolerate defiance, even from a dog.

Somehow, Anton survived the blast and woke up the next day in the village's infirmary. He had cuts bruises, a severe concussion, and a broken leg. He had been very

lucky. First responders attended to him quickly. As for Leo, all that was left was the woven dog collar Nina made for him. Sofia was shocked to hear about their house, but it could be rebuilt. She was most thankful Anton had survived. In fact, he would join them in Poland, since with his wounds, he could not care for himself.

Nina wailed into the night. She could not imagine life without her little pal. She was sure he still must be alive somewhere. Nina had held up through this ordeal, but losing Leo sent her over the edge. She turned inward and became sullen, quiet, and hardly spoke. Her eyes were red from crying. She barely touched her food. Sofia was worried and prayed seeing her daddy would pick up her spirits.

LEO

The two of them were there when Anton's train arrived in Poland. They easily picked him out, stumbling along among the throng of exiting passengers. They rushed up. Sofia gave him an enormous hug and Nina squeezed his good leg as hard as she could. She tried so hard to be happy. Their family was together again. If only Leo were here. Her tears erupted at the emptiness she felt.

As they started toward the station, daddy hesitated and looked back at the rail car, as if he had forgotten something. Sure enough, a conductor appeared carrying some sort of suitcase or bag. He approached them and said, "I think you forgot this." He set it on the walkway.

Nina glanced at the carrying case. Her heart leaped. She saw two black eyes looking up at her through the wire mesh. The whole thing moved as an out-of-control tail wagged against it. Then came the loudest beagle howl ever.

"Leo! Leo!" Nina screamed and snapped open the case. The excited pup leaped into her arms and covered her with sloppy kisses.

"What happened? I thought we'd lost him?", Sofia asked.

"So did I until just before I was to get on the train. It was a miracle. We were sure he'd been obliterated by the tank blast. But a few days later, he came crawling out of the weeds again. He has some scrapes but seems to be the same old Leo. In fact, when the townsfolk heard what he did, he became an instant hero. He had the guts to do what the rest of us would not. There is talk of a statue, renaming a street, or even the entire village. How does Leovia sound?"

They all smiled.

"I am never letting you out of my sight again", Nina said. "You took on the entire

Russian army. No telling who is next."

Leo got it. He looked up at her with those dark eyes, with his best doggie smile on his face.

Why I Wrote this Story:

It is difficult for me to believe in today's world that one egotistical despot could wreak such terror and destruction on an otherwise peaceful people. In writing this story I wanted to humanize this sad situation. As I contemplated how I might do that, as a dog lover, Leo jumped right into my lap.

Flashover in Vegas

Patricia Taylor Wells

Sully Filmore was a wealthy cotton farmer from Yazoo City, Mississippi. He and his wife, Frankie, traveled frequently and were regular passengers aboard the Delta and Mississippi Queens, which crossed up and down the Mississippi River between the Port of New Orleans and St. Paul, Minnesota.

But this year, they would celebrate their fiftieth wedding anniversary, and they wanted to go somewhere they had never been. Sully and Frankie finally decided on Las Vegas, Nevada, and booked a room at the MGM Grand Hotel, which had opened in 1973 as the largest and one of the most luxurious state-of-the-art hotels in the world.

The couple flew out on November 20, 1980. Their anniversary wasn't until the twenty-second, but they wanted plenty of time before and after to enjoy the entertainment offered on the Las Vegas Strip.

Sully always stood out in a crowd, especially when he wore his navy-blue blazer topped off by a neat, red bowtie. His thinning hair was combed back, Anthony Hopkins style. And even though he appeared somewhat dignified, one couldn't help but sense a bit of the devil in him.

After checking into the MGM Grand on their first evening, Sully and Frankie had dinner at one of its upscale restaurants. Tired from their long flight, they went to bed early.

Around 7:00 a.m., there was a frantic knock on their door. Frankie was still getting dressed, and Sully was busy adjusting his hearing aids while trying to figure out the loud noise that sounded like helicopters hovering over the hotel.

Sully opened the door, startled to see a barefoot woman with wet hair and only a towel wrapped around her middle.

"There's a fire," the woman screamed.

"I didn't hear any alarms," Sully replied.

"There weren't any!" The woman's voice grew even more high-pitched. "I ran out of my room without my key and got locked out."

"Get inside." Sully could now smell the smoke that had begun to spread via the return air plenum, stairwells, elevator shafts, the HVAC units, and the seismic joints of the building.

Sully opened the closet, pulled out his new, expensive suede leather coat, and handed it to the woman as Frankie came out of the bedroom to see what was happening.

"There's a fire," said Sully. "Probably just a kitchen blaze; otherwise, they would have sounded the alarms."

"I don't think so," said the woman. "I saw a big cloud of smoke rising past my window. We're on the tenth floor, and that's pretty high up."

The 26-story luxury hotel had three wings built over a casino, restaurants, showrooms, and a convention center. Many of the guests in the hotel's 2,076 guestrooms were still sleeping or unaware that a fire had been raging below inside the building's belly for nearly an hour.

"We're going to die, aren't we?" Frankie looked over at Sully.

"Don't talk like that." Sully scolded his wife. "Tomorrow's our anniversary, and we've made it this far. I promise you; we're not going to die."

"Oh my God," said the woman, pointing to the smoke seeping under the door.

"Fill up the tub," said Sully, "and soak some towels."

As Sully began closing the heavy draperies to help seal the windows, he saw glass raining from above. Although the emergency responders had already contained the fire, the hotel towers were like a chimney, drawing smoke and toxic fumes into the upper floors. Many of the guests, Sully assumed, were breaking out windows to escape the heat and smoke in their panic, not realizing that they could be tragically met by the smoke outside the hotel that was being sucked in through the broken windows.

After placing the towels around the bottom of the door, Sully, Frankie, and the woman sat quietly, waiting for someone to rescue them; but no one came. And apparently, no one had activated the hotel's manual alarm system, allowing the smoke to continue racing up the towers unannounced. Also, the building complex was only partially sprinkled, mainly in the convention areas, showrooms, and some of the restaurants on the Casino level, the Arcade levels, and part of the 26th floor.

"Can the fire truck ladders reach us?" Frankie asked.

"I don't know," said Sully. He walked over to the plaque by the door and read the emergency instructions. Although there were six stairways in the high-rise tower, guests were cautioned that they could not gain access to other floors once they entered the stair enclosures.

"What are we going to do?" asked the woman.

"Well, ladies, I'm concerned about what we might find in the stairways. But we can't sit here, either."

"There're balconies on the other side of the building," said the woman. "My room had one."

"Yeah, but you're locked out," said Frankie. "And even if we got to a balcony, we'd need a helicopter to pluck us off."

"We don't have much choice," said Sully. "We can die in this room or die trying to escape. I vote for the latter."

The trio covered their faces with wet towels and entered the smoke-filled corridor. At the same time, firefighters climbed over dead bodies as they made their way up the stairwell to the tenth floor. Just as Sully passed out and lost consciousness, a fireman rushed into the hallway and slapped an oxygen mask across his nose and mouth. Other rescue workers placed oxygen masks on Frankie and the woman, then escorted them down the smoke-filled stairway until they reached one of the lower floors, where a firetruck ladder could safely evacuate them. If it hadn't been for her dazed condition, Frankie would have insisted on staying with her husband, following him even to her death.

Two firefighters used an ax to break open the door of a room across the hall that had a balcony. They carried Sully outside and signaled one of the helicopter pilots circling the hotel to lower a gurney. After securing Sully to the stretcher, the firefighters motioned for the pilot to lift him from the balcony. Within minutes, Sully arrived at the emergency room and was immediately treated for smoke inhalation. Once they were on the ground, Frankie and the woman were taken by ambulance to the hospital, where Frankie and Sully were kept overnight for observation. The woman, whose name Sully and Frankie never knew, was released later that evening. They never saw her again, nor did she return the suede leather coat Sully had loaned her.

The following day, the LA Times featured Sully, identified as the first victim transported from one of the tenth-floor balconies, dangling from a helicopter lifeline. After being released from the hospital, Sully and Frankie returned to the MGM Grand to examine the damage.

"What balcony were you on?" asked a reporter who had overheard Sully talking about his helicopter rescue.

"Go find the balcony with the biggest puddle on it, and that's where I was!"

From that day forward, Sully carried the newspaper clipping of his rescue in his back pocket. Whenever he checked into a hotel, he would pull it out and slap it on the counter if the desk clerk tried to put him above the sixth floor.

"Not on your life!" he would inform them.

Over the next few days, details about the fire began to surface. Most victims were found above the 20th floor, about as far from the actual fire as possible. Later, investigators determined that the fire began in a hotel deli before it opened for business on November 21. The ignition source was an electrical ground fault inside a wall soffit that powered a refrigeration compressor for a pie case. The vibration of the compressor caused the wires to rub together, then arc due to the friction, resulting in the deli's display cabinet bursting into flames. The pie case was next to a deli bus station where the staff stored plastic utensils and paper napkins. Once open flaming of the bus station took place, the fire was rapidly fueled by the plastic and paper products and combustible materials such as wood, ceiling tile adhesive, and foam plastic padding of chairs and booths. The resulting "flashover" contributed to the dense volume of smoke that had raced up the tower.

Within six minutes, a fireball raced into the casino area, engulfing it in flames. Ten people in the casino were unable to escape and burned to death.

Although Sully and Frankie had planned to go to dinner and a Las Vegas show to celebrate their anniversary, they were just grateful to be alive. They opted to attend a Billy Graham crusade instead. Reverend Graham was on-site during rescue operations and ministered to many of the survivors of the deadly fire.

All victims or their families filed negligent suits against the MGM Grand Hotel except Sully and his wife. As a result, they were awarded a complimentary luxury suite for life after the hotel was restored and had reopened under a new name: Bally's Las Vegas. They did go back once and were given a tour of the new hotel's state-of-the-art fire and safety features. Had these features been in place on November 21, 1980, there may not have been any loss of life.

After surviving one of the worst hotel fires in history, Frankie passed away two years later. Sully was torn apart and died soon after of a broken heart.

Why I Wrote This Story:

My husband and I were on a Delta Queen cruise on the Mississippi River many years ago. There was an elderly couple who were also on the cruise assigned to our dinner table. We were all spellbound by the gentleman's story about their rescue from the fire at the MGM Grand hotel in Las Vegas. The story stuck with me, and I wondered if I could tell it as a short story. I imagined what was said as he and his wife feared for their lives, and I researched how the fire started and why so many things went wrong in such a state-of-the-art hotel.

The Family Trees

Cynthia Darwin

Let me start with that day in the church.

She came in swinging her purse like a Southern church lady, staring straight ahead as a hush came over the crowd in the pews. Her short legs strode like a woman twice her height as she marched to the front of the church and took the urn in her hands.

Turning to the wide-eyed group of mourners, she announced softly in a voice that carried easily to the back of the church, "I'll be taking these with me, if you don't mind."

The befuddled minister stammered, "The ashes, they belong to the family, to his wife."

"As I said," she answered him, "I'll be taking them." And she marched out just as she entered.

In the second row Aunt Lucy whispered to her niece Emily, "You do know the story about the woman he used to meet at the diner, don't you?" "I heard she practices witchcraft," Emily whispered back. "Well, some people would call her a witch," replied her aunt testily.

Four rows back Mrs. Evans looked sharply at her husband, who glanced carefully away. "You said she wouldn't dare show up again," she hissed under her breath.

The woman with the urn closed the sanctuary doors behind her. The younger niece and nephew, parked on the back row for the service, sat up and took note of the proceedings. "Dude! Did you see that?" said Marvin to Esther.

"Wow," Esther answered. "I'm glad we came after all."

The youngest grandson stood up on the third-row pew and asked loudly, "Who was that lady?" His mother Janice, dressed smartly in a black pantsuit and dotted veil, shushed him quickly. The minister cleared his throat, looking to the widow seated on the front row for guidance.

Two mourners turned to each other with sad expressions. "I so hoped it wouldn't happen to her," said one. "It could happen to any of us," replied the other, shaking her head.

The widow began to cry for the first time that day. She gestured to continue the service and the organ played softly. At the gentle suggestion of the minister the congregation bowed its collective head.

Except for me.

I stared at the closed door, remembering the face of the urn thief. Hard to say how old she was. She had that kind of face. And I knew that face.

As the service came to an end I slipped out to my car, avoiding my extended family. I knew the way to Susie's house and had passed it on my way into town yesterday.

The homestead appeared changed from when I left town 45 years ago. The small frame house still stood in the middle of the ten-acre spread. But new paint, a plastic shed and green landscaping gave it a more modern look than when Susie and I had played there every day after school as best friends.

Now trees of differing heights lined the long driveway leading to the house. I turned the car into the driveway just in front of the sign that read **THE FAMILY TREES – *Giving Back to the Community.***

Susie had wasted no time with the urn. High heels kicked to the side of the driveway and a planter's apron over her church clothes, she sprinkled ashes from the discarded urn into the dirt around a new sapling.

She kept at her work, not looking up as I parked the car and walked to her side. "I wondered if you would be at the service today," she said as she patted the earth-ash mix around the tree's roots. "It's been a while....a pretty long while."

"Good to see you too," I replied, looking for that semi-sarcastic tone we had used with each other as companions.

"He was my cousin," I continued, receiving no reply. "I wanted to come for the family."

Susie smiled as she stood up, wiping the dirt off her palms. "Maybe he was family, maybe he wasn't," she said coyly. "Only one way to find out."

"What does that mean? And what's with the drama at the service today, Susie? And all ... all this?" I asked, gesturing to the trees along the driveway.

Many of the trees had an urn mounted in front of them. Others had faded, cloth flowers or a weathered, stuffed animal. A car had stopped at the street where three young women dressed in black stood respectfully until Susie would motion to them.

"People stop by to see their family tree," Susie explained, waving the women in and pointing to one of the taller trees. "Usually after a funeral or some other big event in town. I guess memories get stirred up or something. It makes me feel good to help them, give back to the community."

"And my cousin's family, you were saying? Some question about that?" I asked, glancing down at the freshly planted young tree.

"Well, he was one of Them, you know," Susie answered cryptically.

Confused as I was, some kind of dark understanding began to creep in.

Them.

Mostly football players, some track runners and a few little brothers along for the ride. All young and cocky and drunk. I had fended off more than my share of groping hands and gone home. I was headed off to college the next day. Susie stuck around for the party.

Now I waited for her to explain. "You didn't want to talk about it then and you never came back," she said. "They all had girlfriends who they called the next day to deny being there. And then nobody talked about it again. Nine months later I had Maddie."

No pretense of semi-sarcasm now. I knew about Maddie, even though Susie was right. I never called. That was about the time my parents moved away, headed in separate directions down the highway. I didn't want to talk about that either.

Now I fumbled around with the obvious question. "But, I mean, did you ever try to find out, or I mean, figure out...."

"Really? That was over 40 years ago. As I said, nobody talked. Now Maddie is married, has her own little girl. But I always felt she deserves to have a family tree, like the proper kind on paper with all the branches labeled. And then popular science found me a way to do just that."

That little dark inkling came full forward and I stared at Susie with astonishment.

"You are collecting their DNA samples!"

Susie grinned. "Of course I am. It's no secret, although nobody talks about that any more than they talked about the party. As you know, that's just the way this town rolls."

I stood there gobsmacked.

"But. But, why do they let you do it? Take the ashes, plant a tree that they come to visit? And what about the bodies that get buried?" Too many questions whirled around. "I mean, it's the whole town! What do they tell their kids?"

Susie gestured to THE FAMILY TREES sign. "I've been doing it ever since the first one kicked off years ago. Now, it's an urban legend. Families have come to believe that I do it just for them. Or at least that's the line they tell their kids."

"And it's all legal, which they also know," she continued. "Once I learned how the sample collection and databases work, I began meeting with each of Them to let each one know what I planned to do. To a guy, they asked me to wait until they were gone. But they all signed an official release giving me access to their remains..." she grinned and added, "...however I needed to get them."

"So sometimes I get the ashes and plant a tree. I have to get the ashes before they scatter them, you know, which some people have tried to do. But then I give them a tree in return. Sometimes I show up at the cemetery to plant a tree over the fresh grave, taking what I need in the process. As the sign says, I give back to the community."

Susie saw the shocked look on my face and anticipated

the next question. "Why would the men give me permission? Because they are cowards until the end just as they were in the beginning. Who cares if I cause pain and misery to their family...or families in some instances, which I am finding out... after they are gone? Not their problem anymore."

"And don't get all judgey on me here. If that party happened today, with the right story there are plenty of lawyers and agencies who would get the DNA. Someone would have to own up, provide funds and a name. So, this way, my way, everyone gets to perpetuate the façade and bring flowers to the trees. I'll get what I want."

"So what was the deal with the scene at the church today?"

"Oh," she answered sweetly, "I'm just giving it back to the community." She stepped back to admire the newly planted tree.

After a moment I asked, "Will you provide the results if you get them?"

Susie just smiled. And that's the last time I saw her.

Most people say her body burned with the whole house and line of memorial trees a few years later. The white-hot flames from that hellish fire reduced the whole property to ashes, like there weren't enough of them there already. The fire marshal said investigators were sorting through the dirt samples for DNA results, but "it's more like a mass grave out there than a house fire."

Some of the town folks say the fire was divine retribution. Others say a wronged widow took it all down. And, of course, there is the whole witch theory. But some whisper that the last of Them made sure they all went out of this world untarnished.

I just didn't buy any of those theories. I knew Susie too well.

And my intuition proved correct this morning as my hometown Facebook group blew up the internet. Waves of posts appeared with fresh DNA information that had hit their emails and home pages. Someone had entered new information into the various genetic pages, displacing some time-honored names with that of a neighbor down the street. Or a name appeared that connects a townsperson permanently and without doubt genetically to an entirely different family tree, one no one had ever heard.

More than one person this morning begrudges that cute cotton swab sent on a whim to the international genetic database.

Me included.

I hope Maddie has her proper tree now, but I hesitate to open the email that arrived this morning titled "Your New DNA Matches". Those websites warn that you may find people you didn't really want to find.

Our family trees represent more than just research or cheek swabs, I think to myself. They are our foundation. They are the stories we have all repeated, the songs we know by heart, the happy gatherings, the tearful good-byes. The ancestral eyes we see in the mirror each morning…or think we see. The family branches lift us up. The shared trunk and roots assure us life will go on with the support of those cojoined souls both here and on the other side. And so on…yada, yada.

So, what if it turns out my branch belongs to some other tree, maybe one just next door, so to speak. Like some little bird, do I just flit over to my real tree? Do I perch on the designated DNA branch where I can still hear my shared stories and songs nearby, but only be able to participate as an outsider?

Or does the family tree really make any difference? Does it change anything about you, or the way you would have lived your life? Would one have loved any less fervently? Made fewer enemies? Maybe we should just move forward with DNA blinders, swimming in the certainty of our own familial ignorance.

With a deep sigh I open the email to find out.

Why I Wrote This Story:

Stories write themselves. I believe. The author comes along for the ride with pen or laptop in hand. In the instance of The Family Trees, the opening scene at the church made its way onto my computer over a year ago. While I found it fun and intriguing, I truly had no idea where it came from or where it would go. Over the months that ensued, I took a DNA test for grins and also watched as Roe v. Wade put the question of unwanted pregnancies in the forefront of the news. The rest of the story wrote itself.

The Hurricane

Linda Anthony Hill

'"Robin, move your bike so I can get the Volkswagon into the garage," yelled Bob to his young son as he moved the lawnmower into an opening at the back of the garage.

"I don't know where to put it," yelled Robin in response.

The wind was picking up and they were having to yell to be heard. The hurricane was still many miles out in the Atlantic, but they were already experiencing some of the outer bands. The weathermen were predicting that it would make landfall by tomorrow night. Bob wanted to get everything in the garage now because the winds would get very high before it actually made landfall and they were only three miles from the beach.

"Take the bike out so I can put the VW in," Bob yelled.

"But, Dad, it's my BIKE. I don't want to lose my bike," yelled Robin.

"Don't worry son. We'll get your bike in after we get the VW in. We don't want to risk the VW being blown into the house now, do we?"

Robin complied and Dottie came out to see how they were progressing. "Bob, we still need to go to the store for supplies."

"Make me a list," he yelled. "Have you filled the tub with water?"

"No, I want everyone to get a bath first. It could be days before we get another chance. But all the gallon jugs on the closet floor are filled with fresh water."

"Excellent! Let me get the bug in the garage and then I'll go for supplies. Why don't you go ahead and get the kids bathed? Bill and Marylin will be over in an hour or two and

I'd like to have the tub filled by then." Bill and Marylin lived on the beach and were already supposed to have evacuated. Everyone was concerned about the hurricane making landfall as the tide was high. Their friends might not have a home to return to in a couple of days.

Bob moved the VW into the garage and then carefully placed Robin's bike behind it. He made another pass around the house to look for stray toys or chairs or anything that could become a projectile during the storm.

He went in to get Dottie's list. He looked it over and added batteries. They would need to keep up with the weather reports on the transistor radio if the power went out. six loaves of bread, cold cuts, bananas, four gallons of milk, cereal, bandaids, aspirin, Koolaid, oranges, potatoes, eggs (Dottie would hard boil most of these in case the power went out later), and Tuna fish. Dottie had thought of everything except the batteries and the booze. There would be at least nine to twelve people in the house for at least two days, if not more. Bob would pick up a few cases of beer and a couple of bottles of scotch.

When he walked into the house he could smell that everyone had bathed. They had had bubble baths to help clean up the tub for the emergency flush water. The TV was on and the kids were in their rooms playing. They were excited to be out of school for the next few days.

All three channels were broadcasting the weather situation. The peninsula was being evacuated and they were recommending anyone who lived within a mile of the river also evacuate.

The phone rang. "I'll get it," called Bob. It was another of their friends that lived on the river. Could they come bunk with us for the storm? "Bring your own sleeping bags and food and booze," Bob said laughing. This is going to get crowded, he thought. The house was only three bedrooms with one bathroom. It was cinder block so it was safe, but it wasn't a big house. Still, he couldn't turn friends away when there was a category four looming at their door.

"The McCarthy's are coming over for the storm," he called out to Dottie.

Dottie had just dressed from her shower and made a

frightening face at Bob. "Where will we put everyone? We don't have enough room for ourselves and our own four kids!"

I told them to bring sleeping bags and food and booze. We'll put all the kids in one room and some people can sleep on the floor in the living room. It will be fine.

Bill and Marylin showed up first and then the McCarthy's arrived. They brought lots of goodies and fun snacks, so the kids were happy to share their bedrooms. And they brought cases of beer and soft drinks. The kitchen was getting pretty full.

The wind was really picking up and they heard a tree limb crack and fall in the backyard. Bob ran to the back of the house to check for damage. The roof seemed okay.

The weathermen were recommending that people stay indoors at this point as the outer bands were spawning tornadoes and the band winds were approaching seventy-five miles per hour.

The power went out. Bob grabbed his transistor radio and turned it on. The sound of the wind outside the house was deafening. The radio came on and the reporter was saying that the storm was stalled just off the coast. The best advice was to stay inside and keep listening for more news.

Within a few hours, the wind calmed down, not completely, but it wasn't as horrendous as it had been. It seemed a little lighter outside, too.

"It's changed direction," yelled Bob who had the radio to his ear. "It's moving back out to sea and north. The eye will miss us by at least seventy-five miles if it holds this course. We are on the south side of the eye now." He turned up the radio so everyone could listen.

"The storm is moving away from the coast. We urge residents to remain inside for the night. There is still a high possibility of tornadoes and heavy wind gusts as the southern bands of the storm continue to pound the Daytona area. Cities north of Bunnell to Jacksonville should be prepared to leave within the hour."

The house burst into applause as everyone realized that they had dodged a bullet. "Well," said Bob "we're all here and there's plenty of food and booze. Let the hurricane party begin."

As if on cue, the lights came back on.

Why I Wrote this Story:

I remember several hurricanes from my youth. Some hit, some missed. Either way, it's an experience one doesn't forget. I wanted to share this experience with those who had never lived through a hurricane, so they might have a child's perspective of the event.

An Employee's Fantasy

Linda A W King

Frank Forward loved his life. He loved his job. He loved his wife. He was pretty sure he loved his wife more than his job. Yet, it was an excellent job, and Art Sandstrom was the best boss he could imagine. Everything was good except the Gulf Freeway commute, and with Mozart's help, the drive usually was bearable.

Despite his pleasant life, a restlessness gradually was returning. He knew he couldn't ignore it for long, or it would become a dark cloud chasing him and eventually enveloping him. It was time to move on, his feelings told him, but he now his job was so specific, and he liked every aspect of his project.

He supervised the best department in his company although the insecurity was not for everyone. His staff worked toward building homes compatible with the Houston area environment. Nearly half of his staff were architects, and the other half were a mix: some boat designers, some engineers, and a cable designer. The concept was simple. A home essentially was a barge resting on a support structure. As an area flooded, a home would rise with the flood waters, but it would not drift because cables securely attached to the home at strategic places would uncoil allowing the house to float right above the support structure. Now, they were at the stage of testing models in a weather chamber. The tests included high wind conditions like during a hurricane.

So far, the company had a contract with the City of Houston to make medical and rescue barges to be placed strategically around the city. His company had the option of cancelling the contract if the project were deemed unworkable. Frank certainly didn't want that to happen.

His company fortunately had other sources of income, a line of environmental products and building materials for homes and businesses. Another architectural department provided a steady source of income through designing and building homes on stilts made with fiberglass composite material, using plenty of their green products. The stilted homes would provide protection from hurricanes and rising water in most instances unless the flooding got worse over the years. He often visited that department to get ideas. One idea was a glass floor to take advantage of the stilts and enjoy a garden below, a garden that was happy not to be in direct sunlight.

Frank's office was right across from Sandstrom's, and he got a good view of most things that went on except when a highly placed employee closed the door. Sandstrom worked so hard, and members of top management dropped in on him all the time, all smiley faced, each with a stack of papers.

One day Frank tapped at Sandstrom's open door. "Got a minute," he asked.

"Sure."

"It's not any of my business. I'm being presumptuous."

"Sit down," Sandstrom said invitingly

"On the flow chart, you manage the floaties and the stilts." That was an affectionate term for his department and the architectural department that built the houses on stilts. "Yet, you're always so busy."

"If I only supervised these two departments, I'd have hardly anything to do. You and Dave run your departments with little need for my help. I also work on special projects."

"But you have so many of them." Frank had stepped out of bounds. He couldn't say he thought the top bosses took advantage of him, but he said it anyway.

Sandstrom quietly studied him before he replied, "You're concerned that I'm overworked."

"Well, yes, I guess I am."

"That's the nicest thing anybody has said to me today."

Sandstrom chuckled. His eyes twinkled, and he seemed amused at the very idea of being taken advantage of by top management.

Frank didn't understand Sandstrom's sense of humor. Sometimes he was amused, and Frank had no idea why.

When Frank stood up to leave. Sandstrom said, "You do a good job with your people. You don't mollycoddle them, yet, you're fair and don't show favoritism."

"Thanks."

"You're training your two leads nicely, too."

Frank liked the appreciation and dreaded leaving such a company.

To relax Frank scanned the company newsletter quickly and then pressed the delete. Then he undeleted it. There was something important that he had scanned past. He carefully read the sections again, and nothing looked unusual.

Then he saw it. Under the job listings, there were four. The company liked to fill jobs internally, when possible, even the high-level ones. He found what had been in the back of his mind, Director of Research and Development. That was three levels above him. His boss Sandstrom could do it. Then like a flash, Frank realized that he could handle the job, but how could he possibly be considered.

Yet, it wouldn't hurt to do a resume. At lunch time, he searched through his computer files until he found the folder of all his earlier resumes. He whipped up a first draft, working off his latest one from three years ago.

It was several days before Frank looked at his resume again, but in the interim it did not leave his thoughts. How audacious, he thought. He couldn't do Sandstrom's job, and that was only one level up. Yet, he could easily do Sandstrom's job as described on the flowchart, but he didn't know what the other things were. How could he possibly think he could handle a job two levels above Sandstrom? But still, he studied his first draft of his resume and fleshed it out, emphasizing his group's accomplishments and his contributions.

The deadline was drawing near to apply. He would do it. He would apply, but he would not leave Sandstrom out of the loop.

When Sandstrom seemed totally relaxed, Frank asked, holding a folder with his resume inside, "Are you busy."

Sandstrom invited him in.

"There's an opening for the director of Research and Development. Have you considered applying?"

"That's thoughtful of you, but I need to be right here in this job at this time." Sandstrom studied him a moment. "Okay, let's see your resume," he said, pointing to the manilla folder.

Frank was surprised. He took a deep breathe, pulled the resume out of the folder and handed it to Sandstrom. "How did you know?"

"I'm supposed to know things like that." He read the resume twice. "This is pretty good."

"I'm open to suggestions for improving it."

"No, it's good enough. Send me the electronic copy. I'll add a few comments and send it upstairs."

"Now, who will replace you?"

"Loretta totally can take over. She's very competent and thorough. She is also kind but firm, a good leader." The words just popped out. He hadn't been thinking that far ahead but more to whether he should apply or not.

Later, Frank played the whole interaction over again in his mind. "Now, who will replace you?" That was peculiar. Sandstrom was precise in his language. He didn't say, "Who would replace you."

A few weeks went by, and Frank didn't hear anything. He rather expected an e-mail or letter thanking him for applying and then giving a reason why he was not qualified. Meanwhile, the weather chamber tests were going well, even better than expected.

Out of the blue, he finally got an e-mail from the current Director of Research and Development. "The decision makers will be available tomorrow. Call my assistant to make an appointment."

That evening, Frank pulled a standard list of interview questions off the internet. That helped him feel a bit prepared. The next day, he interviewed with four people.

"You seem to be quite a job hopper. Looks like every

three years."

Frank thought it would be better not to wait for a question. "I'm older, now, and I'm married." Frank tried to look calm and relaxed.

Fortunately, the interviewer moved on.

The last interviewer said, "Our CEO needs to make the decision."

Frank asked, "When will I speak with the CEO?"

The interviewer seemed confused. He frowned and made direct eye contact with Frank. "You're certainly not very perceptive, are you?"

Frank treated it like a rhetorical question and did not to answer. He did not pursue if he would interview with the CEO. Did the CEO always interview director level candidates? Was that something he should know?

He was as preceptive as anyone else, probably more so. Overall, he thought the interviews had gone well but not perfectly. He still might be in the running for the directorship.

Several days went by and he heard not a word. In a way he didn't want to know. He kept wanting to feel good.

One afternoon his wife Jorene called. "Want a traffic report?"

"I guess it's not good."

"There's a three-hour delay on the Gulf Freeway. A car's hanging over an overpass, and the traffic's being directed to the access road. A chunk of concrete fell on a car below, but the driver escaped injury."

Frank would stay downtown if he could get a decent rate. He checked the last-minute hotel websites. Nothing was available downtown. On an off chance, he stopped at Sandstrom's office and asked if he knew of any downtown hotels.

"Come home with me. I'm by myself tonight. My wife is out of town, and I've been meaning to talk with you."

After appropriately mentioning he did not want to impose, Frank accepted the offer.

"Meet me at the front entrance at 5:30."

"Frank was there at 5:15. He stepped outside into the heat. A very fine electric car waited at the curb with the driver standing on the sidewalk. On the car was printed "A. Green Architectural and Supply Corporation."

At exactly 5:30, Sandstrom slid into the car, and Frank merely said, "Nice car."

In about eight blocks, they drove past his favorite restaurant and circled to the side of the building where an elevator took them to the sixth floor. Frank and his wife Jorene longingly had toured a condo in this building.

Sandstrom's condo was nicer with awesome views of downtown Houston. Frank recognized many items that their company manufactured. He admired the kitchen counter tops made from reused glass, then polished, buffed, and permanently sealed. Sandstrom took him on a tour and Frank did not withhold his enthusiasm. Sandstrom's office looked quite large and elegant for a home office. "We bought this condo preproduction and chose everything from the floor plan to the interior building materials. Nothing gives off toxic fumes."

Sandstrom suggested ordering dinner from the restaurant downstairs and Frank resisted mentioning that was his favorite restaurant.

They talked about the weather chamber tests and how the models were holding up.

After dinner, they chitchatted about events going on downtown. Almost out of the blue, Sandstrom said, "I won't have my job forever. I'll need someone good to replace me."

"I'd be honored to be considered," Frank softly said.

"When the time comes, I'll keep that in mind."

Feeling that he had been too forward, Frank said, "I don't know half of what you do."

Frank wondered if Sandstrom's job was the dangle of a consolation prize for being declined for the directorship. And would Sandstrom even know if Frank wasn't going to be offered the directorship.

"Let's step into my office. There are some things I would like to show you." They sat side by side on a white leather couch that faced the desk. "How do you think your interviews went for the directorship?"

"Pretty good, not perfect."

Sandstrom picked up a remote and a screen to the left of his desk lit up and then a screen to the right lit up. "They certainly asked in depth and good questions, I think."

"Did they leave anything out, or would you like to add other information?"

Sandstrom had been good to him. He had to tell him. "There's one thing." He was going to blow everything if he even had a chance for the directorship, but he had to do it.

"I didn't tell the R&D director everything and he asked, too. About every three years I get restless. I feel it is time to move on and I don't know why. That's why the directorship position sounds so appealing. Somehow, I know I can do the work. I have visited all the departments under the director many times, and I know the work of each department."

Frank wanted to say something else, but he didn't. It would sound obsequious. *You're the best boss I've ever had. This is the best job I've ever had.*

"I liked my previous jobs, too. I didn't want to leave any of them, but the restlessness grew so strong. It was like a dark cloud chasing me."

"Here, let me show you a few things," Sandstrom said and clicked a remote. The screen on the right filled with words, like the script from a play. Frank started reading it. It was the transcript of his interview with the R&D director.

Director: You seem to be quite a job hopper. Looks like every three years.

Frank: I'm older, now, and I'm married."

Those two lines of the transcript were circled with a handwritten note in the margin. "He's hiding something. Can we find out what it is?"

Then the other screen came to life. It was dated three years ago, a month before he started his current job with A. Green. It was a standard reference check form from two employers ago. Under the rehire question was a big fat question mark. Below was this: "Excellent architect. Dedicated to his work. Plays well with the other children, but he will leave you and break your heart. You'll never know why.'"

"Wow," Frank said. He was sorry he had read that. "I knew he was upset when I left."

Sandstrom said, "I noticed that you were getting restless, and I wanted to talk with you about it before you found another job and fled."

"I didn't know it showed, I mean the restless feeling."

"It was very clear to me."

"So, they assigned you to find out, like one of your many tasks."

"Something like that. I get restless, too."

"You do? How do you handle it?"

"I developed a way to protect myself. But enough on that."

If Sandstrom didn't want to discuss it, Frank certainly wasn't going to push.

"Do you want the directorship position?"

"Very much so," Frank replied without elaborating.

Sandstrom closed the file on the screen and opened another. It took Frank a moment to realize it was an offer to him for the director's position, complete with the salary listed. The completed letter had been in the computer all along. Frank didn't know what a director should earn, but the amount seemed generous indeed.

I'd like very much to accept this position," Frank said, trying to keep his tone even and to not grovel.

"Then, it's a done deal. Welcome to upper management."

"I'll do my best job possible."

"I know you will."

Sandstrom pressed a button on his remote, and a printer behind his desk threw out the document. Sandstrom retrieved the document and handed it to Frank. Frank read it carefully and signed. He wouldn't have to leave his company. To himself, he said, "Good-bye, dark cloud. See you in three years."

There was the signature spot for A. Green. Sandstrom said, "I'll take care of getting this signed."

The guest bedroom was small but elegant, and the bed was like a cloud, a good cloud. After such an evening, Frank figured he wouldn't be able to fall asleep. But he didn't have any trouble. Maybe it was that delicious dinner in his belly. Or the end of the dark cloud.

He woke in the middle of the night to the street sounds below, a car slamming on brakes, the doppler effect from an ambulance. His thoughts were running in all directions. Something peculiar happened last night. What gave Sandstrom the authority to make the job offer?

A most peculiar thought crossed his mind. That though was the final piece of a jigsaw puzzle. He was drifting back to sleep and maybe he wasn't thinking clearly. Or perhaps his filters were down, and he had figured out something that was right in front of him all along. The finance director had said he wasn't perceptive. That was what the finance director meant. "Will I meet with the CEO?" and the finance director seemed surprised. Maybe he already had met with the CEO.

He awoke to the smell of coffee.

"Do you like frittatas? We also have cereal."

"Frittatas sound wonderful." Frank said. "May I help."

"I've got it under control."

On the table was the contract signed by A. Green in green ink. "I see the contract is signed."

"I have the authority to sign."

Frank resisted saying, "Of course you do."

Once they had finished the frittatas, Frank couldn't resist any longer. "You're Green. Green is Sandstrom. Sandstrom is Green."

The man said, "Allow me to introduce myself. I'm Art Green, also known as Art Sandstrom."

"It's an honor to meet you," Frank said.

His thoughts were spinning. The dark cloud was a good thing. It led him to take action. It led him to this company. It led him to this moment, and now that it wasn't needed, it silently blew away.

Frank said, "The dark cloud was a good thing. It led me to this moment."

Green replied, "The dark cloud is just a cloud. It's what you do with it."

At that moment, Frank realized he had a lot to learn. He hoped that Mr. Green would continue being his mentor.

Why I Wrote this Story

As water rose inside our home and furniture floated around us, we rescued what seemed important until morning when two neighbors in a large canoe rescued us. My flood experience plus my interest in climate change and in mental health led me to write this whimsical story about an architect designing flood-proof homes for the Houston area environment. But the architect is having problems of his own.

Make A Wish

Mary Ann Faremouth

Standing at the foot of the Trevi Fountain in Rome, Louise smiled tremulously. She was awed by the fountain's majesty, but it was the memory of her late father that filled her eyes with tears and her heart with love.

"Every time you see a fountain," he used to tell her, "toss in a coin or two and make a wish. It will bring you good luck."

Good luck! Louise scoffed silently, digging through her purse for a tissue and a few coins. *What I need is a miracle.*

Every area of her life was in turmoil: Her marriage of twenty-eight years had grown loveless and boring. Her long-tenured job no longer offered her a challenge, and the company had no better opportunities for her. To top it all off, her best friend had just recently died of a massive heart attack. Louise felt like the goddess Hecate, poised at a crossroads, a host of decisions to be made laid out before her.

The moment she had found this affordable one-week Italian cruise, she bought one ticket just to get away from everything and clear her head. When she told her husband, he just muttered a reply and returned to his work. Jack was always staying late at the office, and he never expressed much interest in traveling.

When bad weather had their cruise ship stopping in Rome first instead of last, Louise decided to not to bother telling Jack. He couldn't have cared less.

Shaking her head to dismiss the depressing thoughts, Louise exclaimed in triumph as the search through her purse proved fruitful. After drying her tears, she closed her eyes and tossed her coins into the fountain.

I wish I had a life full of love and new beginnings.

"Excuse me, *signora*," said someone behind her in a deep, strongly accented voice. "Would you be interested in learning the correct way to throw coins into the Trevi Fountain?"

Startled, Louise spun around. She vaguely wondered who would criticize how someone else tossed coins into a fountain, but the thought faded when she spotted the personification of tall, dark, and handsome behind her. Salt-and-pepper hair framed chiseled features, and a charming smile revealed a pair of bewitching dimples.

Entranced, Louise could only nod mutely.

The charming smile deepened, and the man stepped up beside her and turned so his back faced the water. "Legend has it that turning your back and throwing a coin over your left shoulder into the fountain guarantees you will return to Rome." He mimed the motion as he described it, though Louise could barely look away from his face. "The tradition dates back to the ancient Romans, who threw coins into the water as offerings to the gods, that they might favor their journeys and help them return home safely."

Taking a deep breath, Louise licked her dry lips. "Thank you. I appreciate the lesson." She hesitated a moment before giving in to the urge to return story for story. "My father always insisted that wishes made at fountains could come true, but he never told me there might be certain protocols."

The man's expression grew gentle. "Well, then it's my pleasure to continue such a fine education." He offered Louise his hand. "My name is Roberto Carruci. I own an art gallery a few blocks away."

Her eyes widened as she clasped his outstretched hand. "An art gallery? How lovely! To be surrounded by art all day—oh, that sounds amazing!" The next moment, she flushed as she realized she was still holding his hand and hadn't even reciprocated the introduction. Clearing her throat, she offered a shy smile. "I'm Louise Forrester, by the way. I just came in on a cruise ship early this morning, trying to get away from the daily grind in Houston so I can try to relax."

Roberto smiled warmly. "Well, then, maybe I can help you with that. My gallery will be debuting some new art this afternoon. I'm headed to a nearby café to meet with the artist right now, but why don't you come to the showing as my guest. Surely, there's nothing more relaxing than Italian art, wine, and nibbles."

Louise could not believe her ears. "You would—" She shook her head, refusing to question her good fortune. "I would love to come to your art exhibit. When does it start? Is there a required dress code?"

"It starts in two hours, and your current attire is perfect." He reached into his pocket and pulled out a slip of paper. "Here's a free pass. It has the details of the gallery's location, and if I'm not there to greet you immediately, this will let you get past the attendant at the door." After what felt like a heavy pause, he added, "Will you be coming alone?"

"Yes, I will be coming to the event alone." She carefully didn't mention that she was *traveling* alone. It was always better to be safe.

Once they'd parted ways, she ran back to the cruise ship to freshen her makeup, spritz her wrists with her favorite sensual perfume, and dab it on her neck. She felt like a teenager about to go on her first date with the handsomest guy in the class.

She laughed at the ridiculous notion. Roberto was probably married to some gorgeous Roman goddess. Still, she was thrilled just to have the opportunity to attend such a fun event.

Ready with time to spare, she headed up to the cocktail deck to settle her nerves with a glass of wine. The coming adventure promised to be fun—just what the doctor ordered to expand her happiness quotient—but she couldn't help but hope for more than she probably should from the event.

She briefly considered calling Jack to at least share her excitement over the chance to immerse herself in beautiful Italian art. However, the memory of his complete disinterest in her trip decided her against it.

Before she knew it, it was time to leave.

As she approached the address listed on the pass Roberto had given her, she spied a long line leading up to the door of the art gallery. Feeling giddy, she quickened her steps to reach the end of the line. She wasn't in line long before Roberto came over, wrapped her in a big hug, and kissed her on the cheek. As he pulled away, Louise couldn't resist tugging him back in and pecking him on the lips. As his eyes went round as saucers, Louise wondered if that had been a bad move, but the smile he flashed her seemed wider than ever.

The gallery was lovely! The walls were hung with amazing watercolors of all sizes. Roberto introduced her to the artist as a dear friend he had met at the Trevi Fountain, which startled Louise. *Dear friend?* They had only met a few hours before. Yet she liked the sound of it and didn't bother correcting him.

The next few hours passed in a whirlwind of introductions, art, and wine. At some point, Roberto began kissing her neck and telling her how nice she smelled. It was intoxicating, a welcome reprieve from the mire her life had become.

Perhaps that was why it took Louise a moment to recognize the familiar man who walked in with a gorgeous young woman on his arm while Roberto was engaged with several other guests. Only as the newcomer's eyes met hers and the color drained from his face did his identity really register.

It was Jack. Her husband.

"Louise? What the hell are you doing here?" he demanded. "I thought you weren't scheduled to dock in Rome for another seven days. Was that a trap?"

At first, Louise could only stare at him. "A trap?" She looked at the young woman on his arm, who looked more confused than anything else, and her mouth tightened. She turned her frown on Jack. "If you think this was a trap, then I'll gladly consider it divine intervention. Is this why you were always staying late at the office?"

A soft sound drew Louise's gaze back to Jack's companion. Though her hand was still tucked into Jack's elbow, she'd taken a step away from him, and her wide eyes darted between him and Louise. Louise's expression softened when she noticed the horror growing in the young woman's eyes.

"I'm guessing this cheating piece of shit didn't tell you he was married."

Red flooded the young woman's face as she shook her head and ripped her hand from Jack's grip. He made a grab for her arm, but she'd already turned and was striding quickly for the door.

Jack called after her before turning back to Louise. "Now why'd you have to go and tell her that?"

Louise stared back at him coldly. She felt like Oceanus's chariot, as depicted in the Trevi Fountain: pulled by two horses, one wild and one calm. On one hand, she was shocked and appalled that Jack had been cheating—probably for years, considering how long he had been using work as an excuse not to come home—and disgusted with his attitude. On the other, she was relieved to know who he really was, and she calmly accepted that she needed to get out and just move on with her life.

Briefly, she thought she heard her dear father's voice: *"Wishes made at fountains really can come true."*

Louise took a deep breath, straightened her spine, and looked Jack right in the eye. "I think you should leave. I don't want to make a scene here. But understand, Jack, that I will be leaving you when I get home. You've shown me who you really are, and this trip has already hinted at the life I can have without you."

Jack's face darkened. Before he could respond, though, an arm slid around Louise's shoulders, and Roberto settled in beside her. He silenced Jack with an assessing gaze before turning to Louise with a concerned frown.

"Are you all right? Do I need to ask this *signore* to leave? I want you to come away from this event with nothing but lovely memories."

Jack didn't give Louise a chance to respond. His face darkening further, he spun on his heel and fled the gallery on his own.

Louise turned with a smile to the man who had made her feel like a goddess today. She wrapped her arms around his neck, pulling him in for a long, juicy kiss. "Thank you, dear Roberto. All is well. This event has been lovely, and I so look forward to whatever comes next."

Why I Wrote this Story:

Now more than ever, I believe we need to keep our dreams alive and live lives of fulfillment and joy. We need to do what is necessary to become clear on what we want and what might hold us back from getting it. Reflecting on the keen wisdom of my late father, I was inspired to write this story with a powerful message.

Looking for Roots

Dick Elam

Elham, Kent, England

Manicured flower beds. Cultured lawns. The cathedral bells tolled the noon hour. The village from where the first Elam emigrated to the New World.

Corporal Thomas J. Elam slowed his Jeep and drove past the Tudor houses. The stone cathedral ahead rose above two-story white houses bolstered with black wooden frames. Elm trees lined the sidewalks.

T.J. thought, *more picturesque than the area postcards he had found in a Folkestone bookstore, bought, and mailed back home.*

Want my family to appreciate their ties to Elham as much as I do.

T.J. had driven north from the English military base where he was waiting to have enough points to return to America. He looked forward to seeing home in Colorado. And then probably assignment somewhere in the Pacific. Maybe landing in the invasion of their mainland---if the Japanese had not surrendered.

He drove past two women with shawls over their hair, walking and carrying shopping baskets. Tom nodded and smiled at them.

The women looked at each other before they smiled at him. Maybe they thought he had lost his way to Canterbury, the usual tourist stop that was 14 kilometers north of Elham.

Tom returned their smile.

They weren't the first English women to show a Negro

soldier the respect you could earn with good manners. Unlike some brash white GI soldiers, Tom and his buddies didn't make fun of old-fashioned British autos, or outdated plumbing, or even some bad food.

Several British had told him they preferred American black soldiers to their "overpaid, overfed, oversexed and over here" white countrymen.

British women noted that, in contrast to some white GIs, the black soldiers did not cat-call them – something that back stateside could have got my Southern brothers lynched, Tom thought.

Tom had read, posted on his barracks bulletin board, what George Orwell wrote, "the only American soldiers with decent manners are the Negroes."

Tom drove around the village square. Then parked his jeep in front of the Rose and Crown pub.

Before entering the pub, he looked at the outside menu board. Atop the menu a boiled egg, a green salad. Below, Plowman's Lunch. Ingredients for the plowman's lunch would probably include something not sold yesterday. He read a hand-written 'now serving locally grown vegetables.'

After two years in England, he knew that Plowman's Lunch of bread, cheese, onions could also include ham. That meal would last until he got back to his Folkestone base.

T.J. entered, looked around the pub, admired the wooden beams that held the roof above the pull-open doors. Old wood that might have been hewn as far back as the sixteenth century.

He walked past the meeting room on his right to the bar and eating tables to his left. He saw he was early for most lunchtime patrons. Only two men sat at the table near the bar talking to the probable owner. They quit talking when they saw the black Army soldier.

The pub owner laid a towel down. Spoke first. "Welcome, Yank. How about a half-pint on the house?"

The two patrons smiled as Tom walked by their table. The pub owner had already drawn the beer from the tap by the time Tom arrived at the bar. "Thank you, sir. Much appreciated. But you don't have to treat me...."

The pub owner interrupted. "Call me 'Henry.' Special occasion for me. Especially, if you are from that barrage balloon company stationed up north before D-Day."

Tom beamed. "Matter of fact sir, I was a replacement for the men who took the barrage balloons to the Normandy landing. Most of them have been returned stateside."

"Then that makes this half pint even more special." He looked at the sleeve insignia before he added, "Corporal."

The pub owner drew the beer, handed to the soldier, turned to the two patrons.

"Let me explain to you two what's so special about this half pint. Been a while since this pub owner heard about that segregation fight up at Lancashire. Back, Corporal, when some of your opinionated white officers suggested the local pup not serve Negroes.

"Pub owner answered by putting up a sign that read 'White officers not welcome!' And I decided, like the owner up there, that Henry Evans would serve a free beer to the first American Negro soldier who walked into this Rose and Crown.

"Welcome. You're the first one."

The two patrons chuckled. One waved for Tom to take a chair at their table. "Good show, Henry. Glad you're showing a little charity that Malcom and I have never seen. And I'll buy the refill. Yank, I'm Patrick."

He proffered his hand that Tom took and shook.

The stocky man next offered his hand. "And I'm Malcolm. Welcome." He shook Tom's hand and asked, "Where you based?"

"At Folkstone. Sandgate to be specific."

"What's your billet, Lad?"

"I was a reserve added late to the Lancashire barrage balloon outfit that Mister Evans was talking about. I wasn't in the group at D-Day. But was with them in France when Germany surrendered. Most of my platoon had enough points to rotate back to the States. I'm waiting. Had time to visit El-ham. Have wanted to see your village long before they sent us to England."

Patrick leaned across the table, lifted his mug. "We are glad to have you Yanks. Here's to you." The three touched their mugs. Tom followed the others and took a sip.

Patrick raised his left eyebrow, asked. "Why come to 'E-lum'? That's the way most of us say the name. Probably because the fishermen caught eels in the river near here."

Tom grinned. "Yes, sir. I know. I owe you a confession. As my bunkmate told me this morning, I'm just another American in search of my roots. My last name is Elam."

Henry put down his towel and leaned over his bar toward the table to listen.

"As a boy, I was told that 'Robert of El-ham' came to the Colonies in 1638 and settled on the James River, near Richmond. They said Robert of Elham became 'Robert Elam' on the Virginia tax roles. My slave ancestors were part of his farm's property. And you probably know that colonial slaves took the last name of their owner."

The men nodded understanding.

T.J. warmed to his presentation. "Robert didn't own as many Negro slaves as they had on the rich Byrd plantation across the river. Robert kept slaves that he freed or were later emancipated. Their children moved across the United States, some as far west as California.

"The last time my mother heard from Dad's relatives, she was told there are about one thousand Elam families in the United States that are white, and another thousand families are black."

Malcolm asked, "Where's your home, Corporal? You don't have a southern accent."

"That's correct, sir. That's because I'm from Colorado. My grandparents grew up in Kentucky, but they moved west before the war started. My Dad got a job at the steel mill. I lost most of my Grandfather's southern accent in Pueblo's high school."

The Englishmen paused to take a sip of their half-pint. Tom sipped his mug. The pub owner waited for the three to drink before he asked. "What's your full name, Corporal Elam?"

"Thomas J. Elam, sir."

"What's the 'J' stand for, Corporal?"

Tom hesitated. He expected his middle name would get a rise. Usually did.

"Jefferson, Sir."

Henry grinned. "Thomas Jefferson Elam. That's a moniker that must have gotten you a rise or two. I'm guessing your Dad decided on that name."

"Yes, sir. Made me memorize and repeat his declaration as soon as I learned to read."

The pub owner smiled. "And probably told you that Mister Jefferson wrote, all men are created equal."

"Yes, sir. He did."

Henry chuckled. "And I'm betting those Colorado school kids gave you a bit of ribbing."

"Not much, sir. That's because I just went by initials, T.J., whenever anyone asked for my name. Or just 'Tom' if that was enough."

Patrick chimed in. "I've got a pen-pal relative that now lives in America. She dabbles in genealogy. Some of her family left Ireland during the potato famine and her grandfather ended up working in Kentucky coalmines.

"She traces some of her Kentucky neighbor families back to your colonial days. Speculates their ancestors were run out of Virginia because they were Tories during the American Revolution."

Tom nodded. "Our original Robert from Elham may have also refused to fight in the revolution. Some of our family have researched and found Elams who fought in the revolution, but not one Robert Elam."

When he saw the three men exchange knowing looks, Tom thought *I shouldn't have said anything about fighting the British*.

"Pardon me if I have offended my gracious Elham hosts."

The pub owner answered. "Not at all, Yank. We're mighty thankful you Colonials came over to help us protect Elham. Here. Have another half-pint.

"But you best know, we don't celebrate your July the Fourth here in Elham.

####

Why I Wrote this Story:

While researching my historical fiction describing 1945 presidential decisions, I discovered English reactions to American "Negroe" soldiers stationed in Britain during World War II. What if a Black Corporal had visited the pub in Kent where I ate in 1978?

The Wandering Ramp
Patricia Taylor Wells

The day after the hail storm, Shelly went to the attic to look for roof leaks after seeing several wet spots on the second-floor ceiling. She had already called a roofer to come over to inspect the damage.

When the roofer arrived, Shelly led him to the second-floor storage room, which had an open staircase to the attic. There was only a tiny amount of light coming from a gable window. The light switch was on the other side of the attic, but Shelly had to climb over ductwork for the air conditioning unit to get to it. Although it was dark, she was familiar with the layout of the attic. Once Shelly had cleared the ductwork, she walked toward the switch. Suddenly, she felt the floor giving away when she stepped on the fold-down attic stairs, which opened to the second-floor hall below. Shelly struggled to hang onto the edge of the attic floor to keep from falling as the stairs unfolded beneath her.

The roofer rushed over and tried pulling Shelly up through the staircase. After his unsuccessful attempts, Shelly's adrenaline kicked in as she pushed herself upward to the attic floor. After lying down, she raised her upper body and saw her twisted ankle.

"I'm going to call an ambulance," the roofer said. "Are you in any pain?"

"No pain," said Shelly, "but you should probably go downstairs and get some ice or a bag of frozen vegetables to put on my ankle. I also need you to call my husband."

After informing Shelly's husband Gary about the accident, Shelly asked the roofer to go next door and get her neighbor Penny, who was a nurse, to come over. Penny came immediately, followed by a fire truck and an ambulance with six rescue crewmembers altogether a few minutes later. It was almost like a party in the attic when Gary arrived home.

Getting Shelly out of the attic wasn't going to be easy. The emergency crew decided the best way was to carry her down the open staircase on a backboard. They would then have to continue taking her down the winding staircase to the first floor. But first, they would have to pass the board with Shelly on it back and forth like a hot potato from one team to another over the ductwork.

"Whatever you do, Mrs. Greene, don't touch anything. Don't grab hold of the wall or the staircase railings; you've got to trust us. It's important not to lose our balance, especially going down the stairs. Just close your eyes. We're going get you out of here."

Shelly breathed a sigh of relief once she was in the ambulance and on her way to the hospital. The orthopedic surgeon on call set Shelly's ankle after determining she had broken it n three places and then scheduled her surgery for the next day.

"You cannot put any weight on your foot," Dr. Wayne said when he checked on Shelly the day after her surgery. "You'll be in a wheelchair for a good while, and I don't advise you to use crutches."

Gary spent the next two days preparing for Shelly's hospital release. He arranged for a wheelchair and a hospital bed and then stocked food and other supplies. The only thing Gary didn't figure out was how to get Shelly inside the house since all three entrances had steps. On one of his trips to the garage, he spotted the dog ramp that their dog Charlie had used while his torn ligament was healing. But one ramp would not work, so he headed for the pet store and bought a second ramp. His plan wasn't ideal and possibly not that safe since the dog ramps were far shorter than the standard length for a wheelchair ramp. But since there were only two steps going into the back door, Gary decided to stick to his plan.

Gary parked the car, unfolded the wheelchair, and

helped Shelly transfer from the car to the chair. He opened the backyard gate and transported Shelly to the back porch.

"You can't be serious," Shelly said when she saw the makeshift ramp Gary had put together.

"Well, I don't know how else to get you inside. You're going to have to trust me, Shelly."

Pushing the wheelchair up the ramp proved more difficult than Gary had imagined. When it almost rolled back on him, Shelly gasped, fearful that her husband would end up flat on the pavement. Gary gave the chair a final push, landing Shelly inside their home.

"We need a better solution," said Shelly.

"I'll call those two carpenters who did some work for us a few weeks ago."

The carpenters could come over the next afternoon, and by the following day, they had completed a twelve-foot ramp made of pressure-treated lumber. On both sides of the ramp were railings made of 2 x 8-floor joists with a plywood overlay. And even though the ramp was quite sturdy, they bolted it to the concrete patio, ensuring it wouldn't move a speck.

Initially, the ramp was just a safe and convenient way for Gary to get Shelly in and out of the house. Later that week, Shelly's therapist showed her how to go up and down the ramp without assistance and even how to lock or unlock the door. For Shelly, this was independence. She could now go outside with Charlie, and Gary would have less to complain about each time they had to go somewhere now that she could get to the car without his help.

Once Shelly's ankle had healed enough for her to walk, she and Gary started thinking about removing the ramp since it took up a lot of space on the patio and was too heavy and bulky to move without help.

"I thought of something," Shelly said. "Susan Gabriel could use a ramp since her cancer has worsened, and I heard she's now in a wheelchair."

"I don't know," said Gary. "We can't just pick it up and carry it to her. And besides, it was custom-made for our house, and the slope has to be just right."

"I've already spoken to some guys at Susan's church.

They'd like to come by and look at the ramp."

The three men that came over to look at the ramp determined it could be retro-fitted to Susan's back deck but would have to be disassembled and moved in a trailer long enough to fit the ramp's floor

The three men that came over to look at the ramp determined it could be retro-fitted to Susan's back deck but would have to be disassembled and moved in a trailer long enough to fit the ramp's floor.

The men took the ramp apart and transported it to Susan's house on Saturday morning. Shelly, Gary, and several other friends of Susan brought food and drinks for everyone. Dark, threatening clouds began to form as the guys worked furiously to reassemble the ramp, but fortunately, the severe thunderstorms predicted bypassed them altogether. When Susan made her triumphant ride down the ramp, a beautiful rainbow arched across the sky, bringing tears and applause to all who were there.

"You don't know how much this means to me," said Susan when she finally talked to Shelly.

"Oh, but I do," said Shelly. "I'm so glad the ramp did not have to be scrapped, and you will get much use from it."

Three months later, Susan passed away. Soon after, Susan's husband contacted Shelly about the ramp, more or less suggesting she could have it back. Fortunately, the guys who had done all the work disassembling the ramp and putting it back together again knew of an older man in a wheelchair who could only get in or out of his house if someone was around to assist him.

"I bet you never thought your ramp would end up serving others the way it has," said one of the guys to Shelly when he called to inform her that the ramp was about to go to a fourth person after the elderly man moved to an assisted living home and no longer needed it.

"I would have never thought such," said Shelly, "but I'm glad that's the case. Until I was in a wheelchair, I never knew the difficulties people with disabilities face. It makes a big difference if you have the means to maintain some of your independence."

Retro-fitting the ramp as needed for each person who

needed it either temporarily or for the rest of their lives had become a ministry for the men from Susan's church. Although modified multiple times, the quality of the materials used for the original construction assured the ramp's longevity. Once word got out about the project, it became known as the "wandering ramp" and served as an inspiration to all who knew its story.

WHY I WROTE THIS STORY

This story is based on the time I broke my ankle in a similar fashion a few years ago. Like in the story, the ramp made for me was passed on to at least four other people who needed one. I like to think it is still making the rounds, helping others with either temporary or permanent disabilities.

The Story of Arty Isaac
B Alan Bourgeois

This was the first time that I saw such a furry of speculation and interest in a new author's book reveal. The publisher, Creative House Press, had sent out all of the normal ARCs for the press to read giving them enough time to publish their reviews by last week. Each reviewer had something positive to say about the book. There were in fact, no negative comments. Something that you rarely see in the publishing world for a new book and a new author.

At the Book Expo in NYC, they had the red carpet rolled out from the front entrance to a sectioned-off portion of the expo floor, just inside the main door. Signs were all over the hall showing the book cover hanging from the rafters, stationed along the various walls of the lobby, and even in the expo hall. But there was not a single picture of the author anywhere to be found. Not on the publisher's website, not in the various articles of the press, and not here at the Book Expo. This was what caught my attention the most both as an author and as a freelance reporter.

Only when the author had to keep their persona private for security reasons was there no picture associated with the book. This was extremely rare, and usually, someone in the press would find out who it was a year or two down the road, or the author would finally give up trying to hide and announce who they were. But this felt completely different. We have the author's name Arty Isaacs, so we believe the author to be a male. Still, that is all we are aware of. Today, in front of hundreds of people here at the expo and thousands via ZOOM broadcasts around the world, everyone will find out what this author looks like and much more.

The tension in the exhibit hall continues to rise higher and higher with each passing hour. I had arrived as soon as the doors opened this morning to get a decent spot to view the show, and as I found out, so did another hundred people. You could hear the speculation of what the author may sound like, look like, etc. Though the main jest of the conversation was about the novel and how well it was written. Many female readers and fellow authors were amazed at how well the author captured every aspect of the persona of each character.

How well the description of the locations, the action, and everything was captured in such a way that people were amazed at how few words the author would use to describe things. Unlike Stephen King who had a niche for writing at times too much to describe something, this author knew how to keep the reader engaged and to use the right number of words.

When I was done reading the novel, I too had to agree that the quality was great. I felt like I had read a lengthy book like War & Peace in just half the time. Full of understanding, and description without the boresome use of the language.

We were an hour away from the revealing of the author when some workers came into the exhibit hall and began to add a few new signs around the stage. The author had already written and published their second book, with a release to follow within two months.

The crowd hushed as they reviewed the new book cover. I was just as stunned as they were in seeing a new book already coming out. Usually publishing houses would wait two years to release a new novel by the same author. They wanted to milk each one for as much money as they could with a variety of sales and author signing events.

Suddenly the crowd began to chatter louder and louder as we all realized that this new book was in a completely different genre than the first. It was not a sequel, or even of the same genre. The first book was a rom-com, while the second book was a fantasy thriller. Rarely did this ever happen.

Creative House was publishing separate titles and genres within months of each other, but for an author to go into a different genre altogether usually didn't happen until they were well established as an author of several books in the same genre.

I immediately looked for a spokesperson for the publisher, which was not hard to find as that person already had a slew of camerapersons and reporters surrounding them trying to get the answers to the questions as I had.

"Why the release of a new book so soon?"

"Why are you releasing a book in a different genre?"

"Will the author be doing a separate book tours for each book, or only one?"

"Are you afraid of losing book sales with such a quick release of a new book?"

The spokesperson stood there with a smile on her face. The one thing that was easy to do as she seemed to tower slightly above the reporters on the wood box she stood on. It was clear she was loving the attention, the questions, and the speculation that the press was showing. But with all the questions, she simply continued to smile and say one thing over and over again. "The answers to your questions will be given in due time." In other words, she would not be giving any answers, and chances would be we would never get the answers to our questions.

The marketing group for this publisher was enjoying the hype they had created and was milking it for everything they could. I couldn't blame them; it had been well over 30 years since any author had been celebrated to any degree that this author was receiving today.

I stood back and looked at the two book cover signs that were now on each side of the stage. The first one, the rom-com, had the typical picture of a man and a woman standing embraced in each other's arms about to kiss, but not completely ready to give themselves to each other. In the background was a farm with wildlife running about. It was entitled, "*A Farm for Clarrisa*."

The second book cover was of a well-built man almost bursting out of his tight shirt wearing a mix of clothing that could not be labeled for one thing or another, but yet had the feeling of a pirate or swashbuckler from the past, but the clothing was old, modern and futuristic all at the same time. He wasn't positioned on a ship, but more of a craft of some sort. This one was entitled "*Aaron's Adventures*"

Two completely different books in different genres are written by the same author Arty Isaacs. 'Who names their kid Arty these days?' I thought to myself.

The hall was filling up faster in this last hour of waiting. In no time, everyone was squeezed in together looking towards the stage, waiting for the mystery man to appear. What did he look like? How old is he? Where did he go to school? And so many other questions that I had, and so did the crowd as I heard the questions being asked over and over again. The noise from the conversations and questioning rose with every passing minute.

From my standing point, I could keep an eye on the door eager to see the press going crazy when Arty arrived. But for now, they whispered among themselves speculating as much as the crowd was as to who he was.

With a half hour to go, movement at the stage started happening. It was the same workers as before moving the first sign to the middle of the stage behind the table where we believed the author and the publisher would sit. They had a third sign to put up where the first had stood. 'Another book? No, it can't be,' I immediately thought to myself. But it was.

Another book cover entitled, "How to Write a Book" by the same author, Arty Isaacs. 'What the hell?' I thought. 'Is this guy crazy, or is this a joke?' Just as before, the crowd had quieted down to a low rumble as they saw the book cover go up for book three. Almost instantly there was a mixture of laughter and confusion in the voices of the audience as soon as they read the title. The audacity of this new writer to have written a How To book on writing before his first book was officially released was stunning. The crowd had felt and believed it as well.

I listened to the voices as the people began to talk louder and louder. They were confused by this new book, but at the same time, they were beginning to believe that it could be done. After all, the press had hyped up the first book so much that everyone wanted to get their hands on it. Now, with the second book coming out in no time, maybe this author had the secret to writing books. But how? What experience did he have to allow him this knowledge and this competency to understand writing that many authors only got years later in their career?

My gut was begging to turn as it knew something wasn't right. No way would a publishing house put out three books in such a short time by the same author. They must have been holding onto them for years, getting them ready for publishing. Yeah, that must have been it. The author must have written them years ago and spent time working on the edits before submission for print. It's true, some authors can write a book in a short time but spend many months fine-tuning it with an editor to get it just right. That must be the case with this author.

I looked over to the publicist once again and saw that the press was hammering her with questions, but as just before, she stood there smiling and saying that the answers will be coming soon. I watched her for a couple of minutes and began to see her smile fading just slightly. She was beginning to wear down from the bombardment of questions from the press. I can't blame them; we were all wanting answers. This was a first for the publishing world.

I continued to listen to the crowds' murmurs as I watched the door waiting for our mystery author to appear. Time had run out for his scheduled appearance. You could hear the disappointment in the crowds' voices. It was hot in the exhibit hall with hundreds of bodies pushed into each other waiting to see who this person was and to get the answers we all were asking.

Suddenly I felt my phone vibrate in my pants pockets. I tried to squeeze my arms around to get to it as it continued to vibrate. Finally, I was able to pull it out and put it next to my ear. "Hello," I said loudly.

I could hear something on the other end, but not clearly due to the loud noise of the crowd. I yelled into the phone, "Hold on a minute as I try to move to a quieter place." I could still hear noise on the other end, but not enough to hear what they were saying.

I squeezed myself through the crowd as quickly as I could, out the door and down the hall while still asking the person to hold on. Finally, I was far enough away to hear better what was being said. "Bruce, is that you?" I heard the voice ask.

"Yes, I responded. Who is this?"

"It doesn't matter right now. I'm calling you to give you a scoop."

"A what?" I asked not sure I heard the female voice.

"A scoop. The author Arty Isaacs is not real." I stood there for a second not responding as I tried to digest the words she just said. Then I caught my breath and asked her to repeat what she said.

"The author Arty Isaacs is not a real person."

"What do you mean?"

"He doesn't exist." Just as she said that I could hear a roar in the exhibit hall where I had just been. 'Shit,' I thought to myself, he's arrived and I'm missing it.

"Who is this?" I asked as I started to head back towards the hall.

"It doesn't matter right now. He is not showing up because he is not real."

Just as I heard her words, I approached the exhibit hall doors. The crowd had turned from excitement of the day to disappointment. Their faces were sad for the most part, but you could also see the anger building in a lot of faces. I turned to one of the press members and asked what had just happened.

"The author is unable to attend due to flight problems," he told me.

Just as quickly as he said that I could hear the female voice on the phone say, "Flight my ass. He's not real Bruce. I'm telling you, he's not a real person."

"How do you know this?" I asked.

"I can't explain now. I have to go."

"Wait, why are you telling me this?"

"Because you're a reporter and you write mysteries and this will be the best one you ever write. The PR team will keep promoting him as a real person, they will even release a picture of him at the event, but it's NOT real." With that, she hung up.

I stood at the door for a moment as I digested what she had said. If Arty Isaacs was not real, then who's picture are they releasing?

I pushed my way back in to get a view of the stage and there on the back wall was a picture of a man in his mid to late 30s with dark hair, brown eyes, and glasses in his hand as it held his head up in a pose. The features at first looked like he could be Hispanic, but the face and features also gave the impression of a Caucasian, with a nose slightly larger that could have been of African American decent. As I study the image, it was clear that there was not one single element that said this person was of one ethnic group or another. It was clear that the person was of mixed race, which was not unusual in this period. But I still felt that it wasn't the full picture of the author. It wasn't sitting right with me.

I continued to look at the image as the publisher stepped behind the table and sat down in the middle seat, where the author was expected to sit. She was a well-dressed black female with a crown of hair that rose about 5" above her head and wrapped in a bright multi colorful scarf. Her dress matched the colors of the scarf exactly with highlights around the edges and matching pockets. She knew her style and she was comfortable pulling off her look.

"Thank you for coming," she began to say as the audience began to quiet down. "I am sorry that Arty is not able to attend. There was a malfunction with the airplane right after it took off this morning, and we are working on finding another flight for him as we talk."

Ok, that is possible considering how many planes have been grounded over the past year for one reason or another.

"My name is Shanice Tompson, I am the CEO of Creative House Press." She paused for a brief moment before she continued. "We are extremely happy to have published the first book by Arty Isaacs, but as you can see, the second and third book of his as well. I am also happy to announce that in six months, his fourth book "The Deadly Sins of His Father," a murder mystery will be out."

"What the hell,' I thought to myself. 'In less than a year, this guy has published four books in four completely different genres. That can't be right.'

The crowd erupted in conversation as they were absorbing what she had just said. I watched her relax a moment as she expected this to happen and was allowing for it to continue. The disbelief in what she said, or in what they heard, both were the same, but being absorbed by the crowd differently than the press.

I could see the press looking at each other with the same questions I had just given thought to.

Shanice began to talk again, but I had zoned her out for a moment as I grabbed my phone and looked at the number that had just called me. It only said 'Unknown'. Suddenly it vibrated in my hand with the same caller ID. I quickly answered it and held it to my ear. Before I could say anything, she spoke to me. "They will now announce that next year there will be another four books put out by Arty." I stood there as I heard the words flowing out of Shanice's voice. "Next year, Arty is expected to have four new novels out, one per quarter."

"Who are you?" I asked again as I scanned the crowd around the stage. Clearly she had to be here in the exhibit hall, but I didn't hear any background noise on her end.

"I will call you tomorrow to arrange a meeting. Be available, you will want to meet."

"Why not now?" I asked into dead space as I heard the phone call end. Silence only existed on the phone, but my mind was going crazy.

"What the hell was going on? Who is this Arty person? Why a push to get all these books out in such a short time?" I was getting a headache with all the questions I was conjuring up. I pushed my way out the door and was met by the publishers' staff handing out copies of the three new books. I grabbed them and continued towards the exit without saying a word.

I was back in my hotel room sitting in a chair near the window and just looked at the three new books I had set down on the coffee table. With a small glass of Tequila in my hand, I sipped on it and allowed my mind to think of every possible question I had for this mysterious female. But the one question I kept coming back to, is WHY? Why would a publisher make up a fake person?

Within an hour, my mind had relaxed from the Tequila influence and allowed me to fall asleep in the chair. The questions were going to have to wait until tomorrow.

* * *

Why I Wrote this Story:

This is a short from a new unnamed novel that has been brewing in my mind for a long time. The concept is about what happens when a large, unregulated company can do what it wants, when it wants, and how it may effect millions of people.

Cowboy Church

Karen S Coan

In the nearing distance, rain turned daylight into a false nightfall. Dark clouds belched loud with anger. Wind kicked up a lively dust trail from his horse's hooves. He downed his head, holding onto his hat, hoping to make it to the safety of the cowboy church before all hell broke loose.

Drops the size of quarters hit like jabs in a bantam-weight bout as he jumped to the ground at the back door and pulled Raven inside, refusing to leave his trusted mare alone in the storm growing meaner than a Wampus cat.

Wiping moisture from his eyes with his wet sleeve, he started taking the saddle off his horse, wanting the calm of familiar on a day that was anything-but routine.

It started with a misunderstanding. Two cowboys he tried to referee. An old-timer and a snot-nosed kid trying to show the cowboys one way was better than the other. He misjudged the situation, and his left eye suffered the brunt of trying to break apart the clash.

One fight too many was the final say of the rancher, and the three of them were dismissed with a week's pay and a forced handshake, no explanations heard.

A man's word was only as good as the time before it wasn't worth the boss man's time to hear it. He wasn't mad. He was in mid-swing when the three of them were pulled apart. Truth be told, he was rather enjoying the release of his own frustrations. Listening to the two of them bickering for days had grated on his nerves. Belting the two jerks was more than justified by the cheering-on he got from the others.

"Need to confess your sins?"

He didn't know if he was more startled to not be alone or to be hearing a woman's voice. "Excuse me?"

"I can probably get you excused with a few Hail Mary's, but I'm not sure about your horse."

She was a mite of a woman, maybe five feet tall, but barely. She looked about as much like a priest as he did, but he liked her spunk.

"Is that coffee I smell?"

"Just made a fresh pot."

"Mind if I join you?"

"Will your horse be needing a cup?"

"She'd prefer a bucket of oats and a trough of fresh water, if you have that, too."

"There's a couple buckets of rainwater over there, fresh caught yesterday. But, I ate the last of the oats for breakfast," she said without breaking a smile, then chuckled and added, "If you'll call ahead next time, I'll choke down that nasty cream of wheat instead 'til the two of you can get here."

The day starting strange got even stranger, but in a way better way.

He tied Raven to the kneeling bench and followed the young woman through a side door, down some narrow concrete steps.

The small wooden structure above ground was just big enough for a makeshift pulpit with a rickety podium someone built too many years back, the big cross fashioned from an old fence nailed to the wall behind it, less than a dozen simple wood benches, and the heavy front and back doors.

He thought those two doors were for people like him who always needed an escape route. He never thought about a basement.

The coffee was as strong as it smelled, and he pretty near drank his cup before he realized they hadn't had a proper introduction.

"Jasper," he said, as he got up to get more coffee. The sparse room with a bed pushed against the corner reminded him of the old homestead. He sure could go for some of his mama's cooking about now, but he'd make do with the coffee.

He liked she'd made it in a dented metal pot, put right on the flame of the old-fashioned, cast-iron stove.

He didn't like she wasn't returning the favor of her name, so he prodded her with more of his, "Samwell. Jasper Samwell."

When he turned around to offer her another cup as well, he was surprised at the look on her face. It had gone from kind amusement to downright sour. He wasn't sure where this was headed, but he was sure he needed to be on his way.

"I thank you, ma'am, for..."

Before he could make his excuse and skedaddle, she crossed the small space between them and landed a full-hand slap hard on his left cheek, the one still shy from the black eye earned earlier in the day.

His mood dived to match hers, and he stepped back, not sure what he'd done wrong in the short time of her acquaintance but not wanting a repeat of her strong hand. More than that, he didn't want his temper to do something they'd both regret. His daddy taught him to never hit a woman, and his mama made sure he knew there'd be times he felt the need but had to resist temptation.

He braced himself for more of the same, in case that was the direction she was headed. Turned out, she wasn't. He didn't know if he was more startled at the mad of her earlier slap or the deep of her kiss now. How she managed to pull his neck far enough down to meet her tiptoe, he was unclear, but needed a bit more, "Do I know you?"

Her eyes dug into his gut, landing them in a stand-off stare neither wanted to lose.

It wasn't until she cocked her head, in just that way, he realized, he did know her, or someone like her.

The clock stalled, then took off in a cartoonish whirl back through long forgotten years, and the dizzy turned his legs into mush.

"Maggie?" he finally managed, moving his hand toward her shoulder to see if she really was standing there.

"You wish."

He watched as she sashayed an all-too familiar turn-away and disappeared up the concrete steps.

He leaned against the warm stove, needing a pause before mustering the wherewithal to follow her. His head moved from right to left and right again, where it hung in utter confusion.

It couldn't be her. She would be older, like him.

It could be her daughter, he guessed. He did a quick calculation and mumbled, "not possible," as the creep of guilt traveled his recall of the last time he'd seen Maggie.

It ended badly. She got in a couple good pounds at his chest and clawed his face before he stopped her with their last kiss.

That kiss haunted him.

He wasn't about to make that mistake again.

He bounded up the steps, hoping she hadn't let her anger forget the storm raging outside. When a lightning bolt struck too close, he saw her sitting on the last row of the wooden benches.

She was staring at the cross. Hands folded in her lap. Tears streaming down her cheeks. And, his heart fizzled.

He didn't know whether to hug her or yell at her.

Women had always been the bane of his existence, and this moment felt the epitome of all his blunders. Yet, he wanted to know whatever it was she had to say, so he walked toward her in a deliberate slow way to give his curiosity time enough to find the courage to deal with her wrath.

He knew he deserved it, whatever it was, he just didn't know why.

"You'd better sit over there," she said when he reached her, so he did as she wanted and kept quiet, waiting for her. It was a while before she spoke, and her words shredded him.

She had practiced them, he could tell.

They were curt and sliced bits of him into the raw she intended.

The saddle he'd put around his heart slowly unraveled, stitch by stitch, as he listened.

"You broke her spirit, that's what Grandma said. Said she was never the same, after you. Said you ruined her."

The woman, a younger version of her mother except for

the eyes, continued her fixation on the cross, as if looking at his face was disrespectful.

She sighed several times before continuing, "She married my father in a rebound, they said. He didn't deserve that. He was a good man. Loved her more than she ever understood. She was so caught up in you, she couldn't let go. Couldn't move on. She couldn't forgive you or allow herself to be happy without you."

The blood running through his veins broke off jagged icebergs drifting in slush.

He'd never imagined what her life was like, never realized she had to figure a way to make do. He'd only struggled through his own regrets and taken out his disappointment on a trail of women who never stood a chance of living up to her.

How she must've despised him leaving her. How she must've resented him escaping her. How she must've hated him deserting her.

There were no words, no excuses. He deserved more than the slap, but he couldn't understand the kiss.

Even though he should've held true to what his mama taught him about not messing with the fairer sex, he couldn't help but ask, "Why did you kiss me?"

She laughed so hard the echo held its own with the thunder rumbling outside.

Grinning, she showed off a healthy set of teeth as she moved her head from side to side to side, as if stunned he even asked.

Her stone cold glare was worse than the slap.

Darkness from the storm made it hard to tell if day was done. If not for the constant flashes of lightning, the little church would be pitch black. There was no electricity, as far as he could remember. Church happened in daylight, and candles lit the sinners' way to the kneeling bench.

The cowboy church was nondenominational, which made it whatever the lost soul needed it to be. He'd used it for refuge quite a few times over the years when he'd been in these parts for roundups of cattle and even rattlesnakes.

A cowboy's life took him where there was work. All he ever needed was a place to sleep, food in his belly and a use for his hands. He liked going to bed tired and waking early. He liked the smell of dew still on the ground before the sun showed up. He liked campfire food with its ashes and a bit of trail dust giving it substance. He liked his coffee strong, almost scalded. And, he liked the freedom of picking up when he wanted to go to another place until he needed to leave again. It was a solitude he enjoyed. Pass-through friendships. Enduring hardships. Proving he was as tough as he thought he was.

His was a reputation of a short-timer with a short fuse and a strong back.

He prided himself in his fearless approach to getting whatever needed doing done. Volunteering before thinking and earning some pretty impressive scars because of it.

He'd won Raven in a card game, the best hand he ever had. The two of them traveled countless miles with enough distance to be brag-worthy. He liked to think of her as the queen in the corral, putting the stallions and geldings to shame with her boasts.

He looked at Raven now, still tied to the kneeling bench and lifting an occasional glance at the two of them between her obnoxious drinks of water from one of the rain buckets.

Raven was the longest he'd ever been with a female, and that sounded sad in his mind as he thought it.

Much as he didn't want the confrontation with the other female in the room to taste any more bitter than it already was, he knew he owed it to her, and to her mother, to man up.

Even as he said the words, "I'm sorry," he realized his mistake.

Why I Wrote this Story

I'm a dabble-artist and created a drawing of an old abandoned country church with a cowboy riding toward it as an awful storm headed his way. It inspired me to write his story because it needed to be told. When it hits this hard, there's no thinking, just capturing thoughts as they spring from my fingertips onto the pages. In less than two thousand words, the storm grew fiercer as the struggle inside tore the tough old cowboy apart. He was forced to deal with his mistake—an epiphany everyone should encounter at least once in a lifetime, and I hope this story jostles yours as much as it did mine.

The Evil Within

Karen S Coan

Little boy Tommy had stared at that door a thousand times. Never daring to turn the knob and go inside. Never brave enough to cross the street for a closer look. Never sneaking a hideaway in the tall itchy weeds where green grass was supposed to grow.

Standing there now on the rotted front porch, his stomach turned somersaults and both palms trickled in sweat as his throat lost its spit.

On most levels, he knew it was ridiculous to feel such strong emotions all these years later.

A full grown man, he was considered a very successful businessman. He had an enviable reputation as a savvy real estate mogul. This was just another piece of property he'd found online. He was there to do his usual quick assessment of the damage. Calculate the costs. Figure out how to flip the disaster and parlay the profit to purchase more dilapidated properties. The endless possibilities in these initial reveals usually excited him.

And, this house did excite him, but in a whole different way.

"Too late to back out now, chicken shit," he said aloud to no human being around to hear it, then positioned his bolt cutter to demolish the rusted chain guarding the front door. Success renewed his sense of purpose and focused his distraction in a powerful flush of adrenalin.

His first step inside threw him off kilter.

Thrown aback, he glared into the dark, abandoned house for a logical explanation of his renewed angst. It took a moment to discern the clump his foot had found was a squirrel corpse.

Timing is everything.

When the dead squirrel's ghost or a living distant cousin jumped on his shoulder on the way to a large limb of the twisted oak tree crashed into the front porch, he damn near lost it.

"Shit!" his echoed word scattered lounging critters and dispersed creepy bugs into and out of and around cracks, crevices, cave-ins as he sunk into his childhood terror. Countless nights in his twin bed churning all sorts of imaginable horrors spurned by town gossip about the gnarly old man everyone said lived amongst the rotting bodies of his victims.

Two deep draws of breath and one wide head shake, he managed to muster enough courage to push aside embarrassing old fears and proceed anew with his adult project. He had to be back in the city tomorrow night for a meeting he couldn't miss, which gave him a sparse amount of time for his tour before putting in his winning bid. He'd have to hire a local subcontractor who could gather crews willing to take low-paying jobs with impossible deadlines to make his numbers work. Three weeks was his fragile timeframe with no contingencies and no back-up plans. This would either be his best endeavor or his ruination.

He started again, stepping carefully around debris whether dead or alive. Tugging what was left of ragged dusty drapes gave him barely enough light along with his flashlight to be discouraged.

It was worse than he anticipated.

Half the ceiling lay in heaps on the first floor. Every wall was riddled with holes punched by vandals, and vile graffiti covered everything. Around each and every turn was a scattering of drug paraphernalia and a disgust of stained mattresses. The wretchedness of the stench overwhelmed the senses.

Yet, it was the kitchen he found most appalling.

The sink and countertops were unrecognizable with their overflow of broken dishes, nasty pots and other things he didn't care to get close enough to identify. Flies and cockroaches had taken up residence, which meant some of the mess was new. Rumpled fast food bags looked no more than a day or two old.

"Fucking adictos!" He laughed at his own sarcastic joke. He knew precisely why drug addicts flocked to these kinds of places. There were no landlords demanding rent. No families with cold turkey rules. Places like this meant free reign. An open invitation to live in their disgusting cycle of next-fix demise until death relieved them of themselves.

He wished he'd brought his city collection of peons with him. They'd already be knocking walls down to studs. Ready to throw up flimsy wallboard and slap on cheap paint, while he stuck his sign in the yard. Managing quick turnaround superficial flips was his meal ticket.

This squirrelly nightmare was way outside his usual stomping ground, and he was on his own.

It had been too many years since he lived in this small town for him to know anyone or for someone to remember him. His family moved to another state when he was a teenager. He attended college on scholarship in the big city until he fell, literally, into his current career. To distract a naïve college kid barely scraping by from realizing an ambulance-chasing lawyer could turn his mishap into millions, unscrupulous Gordon Philips flimflammed him. Said the significant cost of the trespassed fall into an illegal construction scrap pit could be worked off. Gave him a choice, of sorts. Either accept the old man's pull-up from the pit as a handshake deal, or, let the truck dump his fate.

A self-professed scoundrel with no qualms doing whatever he needed to get his way, Gordon ended up more or less adopting Thomas. A filthy rich man with four daughters more interested in spending his wealth than learning the family business, he took pleasure in grooming and goading his young male protégé. Let him live rent-free in vacant houses. Talked him into dropping out of college by paying off his loans and helping him get his own real estate license. Allowed Thomas to pay him back in debt sweat, giving him the unenviable role of flunky to all the other flunkies.

Thomas did Gordon's worst jobs. He took on the most disgusting tasks. Figured out ways to do things no one else wanted to tackle. Slinked in and out of the shadows, crossing every line, no matter how disgusting nor how illegal. He earned the other men's respect, which they claimed was a knife blade sliver more than the boss man himself.

The payoff was learning the real rewards of hard work and dirty words in Spanish.

Today's tour was far from his worst experience but the surprises kept coming.

The pantry held the remains of a mummified mother cat and her four skeletal kittens mid-birth.

The downstairs bedroom closet was jammed with boxes of old kids' games, bags of small-sized clothing items and a foot locker of little bones, some of which could be human.

The third tread of the creaky wooden staircase had been ripped up and a shoebox of assorted species' teeth that had been kept hidden was spilled everywhere.

Up the stairs, identical bedrooms flanked the landing. Each had sharp-slanted ceilings. Each had identical large black pentagrams painted on the floor. There was a bizarre absence of furniture and debris or any evidence of the druggies. An even more curious lack of dust.

He hurried back to the landing with its oversized window seat and the notorious dormer window.

On his upward trek through blinding sunrays, he'd missed seeing the varied and extremely odd amulets and talismans hanging at different levels from what remained of the staircase's tall ceiling. In a stupid attempt at mockery, he slapped the one hanging lowest that came loose in his hand. The maker's pathetic model of a little boy with red yarn hair bemused him until he realized, when he squinted, it could be construed as his doppelgänger. The thought revolted him. When he threw it out the broken dormer window, something sharp pricked his thumb.

To check his wound, he sat on the oversized window seat, still semi-covered with a tattered cotton cushion, and checked his wound. As he sucked his own blood, he was flooded with the years of his youth haunted by the large candle flickering from this very window each night he and his brave friends sneaked from the safety of their own houses to stare at it.

The tall brass candlestick had long ago been stolen. What remained were dusty clumps and sinister drips of old wax still clinging to the windowsill. He flicked at some of them with his middle fingernail as his thoughts went to a place deep within he hadn't allowed in a while.

A little boy's mind is filled with grotesque fantasies of slaying dragons with bloody swords and killing bad guys with powerful guns. It's also filled with wicked curiosity of what happens behind the closed door of parental bedrooms to produce strangely enticing guttural noises. Over the growth years, curiosity turns into immature experimentation, the kinds of things that worry parents and teachers into huddled conferences. But girls change, too. Channeling the innocence of childhood friendships into teenaged siren bodies. Growing interesting breasts and developing gentle curves that rage the hormones of every teenaged male into lifelong conquests of bad girls to earn bragging rights.

All boys get angry from their frustrations. All boys feel abandoned when punished for acting on their desires. All boys fester in their miseries.

He realized the man who lived here was no different. This house was where he played out his fantasies. Where he tormented his temptations. Carried out his evils.

Looking out the same filthy window where the old gnarly man must've sat. Looking through the same twisted tree limbs. Looking at the same spot where little boy Tommy trembled his cowardice those many years ago.

Thomas didn't have a candle, so he lit a cigarette.

Watching the creep of night.

Flicking his Bic.

Waiting.

Why I Wrote this Story:

When I was a child, I was fascinated by old houses, especially the abandoned ones covered in super creepy cobwebs, tons of sneezy dust and dark secrets. Childish stirrings never disappear, they just get trampled on by life unfolding the day-to-day necessities until something tickles a nerve and unravels an old, fragile thread of imagination unresolved. This story is my drift through a little boy's fears to a grown man's greed that ignites something decidedly evil. Is it the scary house playing tricks on his memories? Is it the old gnarly man's spirit coming to life through his soul? Or, is it just wicked twist of fate unfolding a new sordid tale? Perhaps. Perhaps not. You decide and let me know.

DEAR Indie,

would like to thank our sponsors and our advertisers for helping us to raise money for literacy.

DEAR Indie
Drop Everything And Read Indie

Our Goal is simple: To Encourage Reading for All Ages

Please Support & Donate to our Cause by going to this link:
http://dearindie.org/index.php/donations/recurring-monthly-donations

Introduction

D.E.A.R. was originally a part of a story line found in the book Ramona Quimby, Age 8 (pages 40-41) by Beverly Cleary. The book was first published by Harper Collins children's division and they are the ones that crated the DEAR event that has been a part of schools and libraries for years. Texas Authors, Inc., a not for profit organization was inspired by the concept and added their own Texas touch to it, thus creating DEAR Texas in 2014 and added Dear Indie in 2018.

More About Us

The DEAR Texas concept started with an annual event created in 2014 and then implemented in 2015 when Texas authors were distributed around the state in bookstores, libraries, and schools over a two-day period in April to spotlight their works to readers. The overwhelming response from this event, demonstrated that it needed to be its own separate organization, thus Texas Authors, Inc., moved it out from under its organization and set it up as a separate 501.c.3 in Texas.

Partnerships

Drop Everything And Read is an organization that is dedicated to not only encouraging more people to read, but also to support Indie Authors. We do this by providing Indie Authors books to Title 1 Schools & Libraries across the country.

Since 2011 Authors School of Business has been helping authors to succeed.

We do this through our video and in-person classes, programs, events and other opportunities that give subscribers more opportunities than any other organization in the world.

Our founder has set trends, created new opportunities and refined the meaning of marketing for authors and small press publishers.

With the Board of Directors made up of authors, they work together to make sure they offer the highest quality education while at a sustainable price that helps the author to grow, and to succeed.

Join this one of a kind organization and grow stronger in the publishing world at http://AuthorsSchoolofBusiness.com

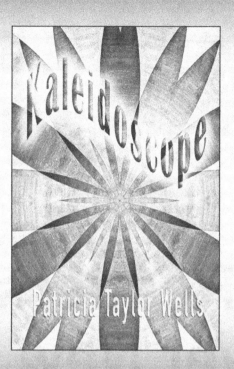

Where Readers Discover New Talent

Where Authors Earn Their Fair Share

CPSIA information can be obtained
at www.ICGtesting.com
Printed in the USA
BVHW092238151022
649525BV00005B/166